This was *no*

Something in her blood responded. He tasted it on her lips, smelled it on her perfumed skin. Suddenly he hated the game; he wanted this to be real.

Raising his head, he let the breeze cool his face. He would have stepped away from her, but the tight space made it difficult. He waited for her eyes to open, then grinned down at her. "I pity the poor man who marries you, my dear."

The saucy smile returned. "I should be deeply wounded by those words, Lieutenant, but with that drawl, you could say just anything. Now, tell me why you pity my future husband."

"Because he'll never be able to let you out of his sight."

The dimples deepened. Her hands went around his neck, pulling him toward her as she whispered, "Why would he want to?"

"Good question."

Dear Reader,

Entertainment. Escape. Fantasy. These three words describe the heart of Harlequin Historical novels. If you want compelling, emotional stories by some of the best writers in the field, look no further.

Cassandra Austin made her writing debut in 1993 with *Wait for the Sunrise*, which earned her scores of fans and set the tone for her tender and emotional Westerns. Critics have described her work as "charming," "enlightening" and "not to be missed." Her latest, *The Unlikely Wife*, is all that, mingled with a delightful humor that only a heroine like the confident, flirtatious Rebecca Huntington can evoke. She is the very unusual bride of army officer Clark Forrester, *and* is his colonel's daughter. Don't miss the sparks flying!

A roguish nobleman and a shy chatelaine forced to wed prove that opposites do, indeed, attract in *The Welshman's Bride*, another terrific medieval story by the talented Margaret Moore. Author Janet Kendall makes her writing debut with *Hunter of My Heart*, an exciting Regency tale about two Scottish nobles bribed into marrying to protect their past secrets.

Rounding out the month is *Maggie and the Maverick*, the last of Laurie Grant's DEVLIN BROTHERS books. Wounded in the war, single dad Garrick Devlin reconstructs his life with the help of a dainty Texas *Yankee* who wins his respect and teaches him to love again.

Whatever your tastes in reading, you'll be sure to find a romantic journey back to the past between the covers of a Harlequin Historical® novel.

Sincerely,

Tracy Farrell
Senior Editor

Please address questions and book requests to:
Harlequin Reader Service
U.S.: 3010 Walden Ave., P.O. Box 1325, Buffalo, NY 14269
Canadian: P.O. Box 609, Fort Erie, Ont. L2A 5X3

The UNLIKELY Wife

CASSANDRA AUSTIN

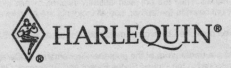

HARLEQUIN®

TORONTO • NEW YORK • LONDON
AMSTERDAM • PARIS • SYDNEY • HAMBURG
STOCKHOLM • ATHENS • TOKYO • MILAN • MADRID
PRAGUE • WARSAW • BUDAPEST • AUCKLAND

ISBN 0-373-29062-4

THE UNLIKELY WIFE

Books by Cassandra Austin

Harlequin Historicals

Wait for the Sunrise #190
Trusting Sarah #279
Cally and the Sheriff #381
Hero of the Flint Hills #397
Flint Hills Bride #430
The Unlikely Wife #462

CASSANDRA AUSTIN

has always lived in north central Kansas, and was raised on museums and arrowhead hunts; when she began writing, America's Old West seemed the natural setting. A full-time writer, she is involved in her church's activities as well as the activities of her three grown-to-nearly-grown children. Her husband farms, and they live in the house where he grew up. To write to her, send a SASE to: Cassandra Austin, Box 162, Clyde, KS 66938.

To Jonathan, Eden and Paul

For all the times you let me write when you would rather
have had cookies. You turned into fine adults anyway.

Chapter One

Kansas, 1867

"The window's so dirty I can barely see out," Cousin Alicia Evans said.

"There's nothing to see anyway," responded Aunt Belle.

Rebecca Huntington's only response to her companions' conversation was a muttered "Hmm," which she assumed they took as agreement. She didn't agree, however. She leaned slightly into the aisle, quite pleased with the view. Since the train had pulled out of Kansas City that morning, she had been keeping close watch on the activities of a very good-looking soldier. His uniform told her he was a cavalry lieutenant. He was clean-shaven, something slightly unusual in the West. She thought his choice to shave could have been vanity; he had the most magnificent jaw she had ever seen, strong, square and well-defined. It would have been a shame to cover it.

He had left the car some time ago and had only just returned, stopping to talk to someone in a forward seat and giving her a wonderful opportunity to admire his profile. One hand rested on the back of the seat as he bent slightly forward. Rebecca marveled at how easily he braced himself against the train's erratic rocking.

He ended the conversation and straightened, turning toward the rear of the car. Rebecca jerked upright but continued to watch. Three steps down the aisle, his eyes met hers. His were gray, quite a charming contrast to the tanned face and charcoal lashes.

She thought his step might have faltered when he caught her watching him, but it could have been the jerking of the train. His face didn't register surprise, even when she refused to turn demurely away. He tipped his campaign hat, and a dark lock slid free to settle against his brow. "Ma'am," he murmured.

Rebecca smiled, well aware that the dimples that appeared in her cheeks had a devastating effect on some men. "Lieutenant."

He didn't stop, and in two steps he was past. Rebecca was wondering what excuse she could use to stand and look behind her when a sharp pain on her knee made her jump.

"Don't do that!" Aunt Belle snapped open her weapon and fanned herself briskly.

Rebecca tried not to scowl. The woman, of course, felt compelled to act as chaperone to both girls. At twenty, Rebecca considered herself fully grown and had for some time. Alicia might need her mother's restrictions, she thought, since she was still a child of sixteen.

"Don't do what?" Rebecca asked, feigning innocence.

Belle hissed, "Don't smile at strange men."

"Oh, Aunt Belle, he's an officer. I've been around them all my life. Most of them are gentlemen." She gave her companion a dimpled smile, afraid it would have little or no effect on her.

"Don't smile at strange gentlemen, either." With this pronouncement of decorum, the older woman returned her attention to the nearly opaque window.

Rebecca wasn't ready to let it go. "He's a soldier. He deserves a civil greeting."

Belle didn't glance at her. "That wasn't a civil greeting."

Pretty little Alicia was eyeing her with a combination of fear and awe. Alicia rarely defied her mother, and she never, ever flirted with men. While the look begged her to behave, Rebecca knew Alicia would be disappointed if she did.

She stretched, a most unladylike activity since it would have been impossible to accomplish if she actually wore the corset the other women assumed she did. "It's quite stuffy in here," she murmured. "I believe I'll take a breath of air on the platform. Would either of you care to join me?"

Both women stared at her. Aunt Belle found her voice first. "Is that safe? Why, the train's moving so fast you could tumble off."

Rebecca blinked innocently. "It does happen occasionally. Still, if one is careful..." She let her voice trail off as if she were doubtful. She looked from one shocked face to the other. "No? Well, I'll only be a few minutes."

She stepped into the aisle and, pretending to take a moment to gain her balance, searched the rear seats for the lieutenant. She was lucky on two counts. He faced in her direction, and he hadn't put his hat over his face to try to sleep. It took no effort at all to get him to notice her. She walked slowly past, smiling sweetly. As she opened the door at the rear of the car, she cast a glance over her shoulder, pleased that he was watching.

Lieutenant Clark Forrester enjoyed the view of swaying hips as the young lady left the car. Her message couldn't have been clearer if she had sent a telegram. He relaxed, giving her a minute to wonder if he was coming. He knew the game. First she must pretend to be shocked at being alone with a man, then she would relent and agree to talk for a few minutes. If he said all the right things, he might be lucky enough to win a kiss.

Of course, if they were caught, she would have to

slap his face and he would have to take it to save her pride. That was the gamble. He didn't have to wonder if it was worth it. No man who had ever been stationed on the frontier passed up a chance to spend time with a woman, let alone a beautiful one. The next chance could be months away.

Deciding he had left her in suspense long enough, he glanced toward her companions. They weren't watching, and he rose, placing his hat in his seat so it wouldn't be blown away, and slipped out the door. The gallant soldier-to-the-rescue was always an acceptable image, he thought, but, before he could express his concern for her safety, she turned from the railing and smiled.

"The hills are lovely, aren't they, Lieutenant?" she asked.

"Yes, ma'am." The hills? The hills were lonely and barren and, though it was only June, already burned to a yellow-brown by the sun. But she was most certainly lovely. "It's hard to even notice the scenery when I have you to look at instead."

"Charmingly said. Come stand beside me so we don't have to shout above the wind." She turned away to gaze at the passing hills.

Clark hesitated. She wasn't following the rules, and it left him unsure of his next move. The wind was blowing, of course; it was always blowing on the prairie, but, even with the constant clatter of the train, in such a small space there was no need to shout to be heard. The edge of the platform with the lovely young lady was only a step away and narrow enough that if he stood beside her, he would be standing against her. He took the step.

"I've been gone for six years. It'll be wonderful to get home," she said. "Where are you from, soldier?"

"Virginia, ma'am."

"I thought I heard it in your voice." She was now directly in front of him, her upturned face only inches away. He wasn't sure how much longer he ought to wait, how much longer he *could* wait.

"And what would take you away for six years and leave you homesick for the prairie?" He put one hand gently on her waist, ready to remove it at the slightest sign that he was acting too quickly.

"The war first. And an education," she said, still smiling.

Clark grinned. Now he knew the game. "Did they teach you everything you wanted to know?"

The young lady shook her head, her smile gradually fading as her whiskey-colored eyes darkened. Time to call or fold.

He lowered his head slowly, watching her eyes drift shut before his lips found hers. He kept the touch as gentle as possible, allowing her the choice of pulling away. When he felt no hesitation on her part, he brought his free hand up to her neck, urging her closer.

Her lips parted sweetly, and her tongue met his. This was *not* the lady's first kiss. But he wouldn't hold that against her. His arms tightened and felt warm, firm flesh beneath several layers of cloth. No whalebone or steel cinched this slender waist. The realization made his pulse leap.

Something in her blood responded. He tasted it on her lips, smelled it on her perfumed skin. Suddenly he hated the game; he wanted this to be real.

Raising his head, he let the breeze cool his face. He would step away from her, but the tight space made it difficult. He waited for her eyes to open, then grinned down at her. "I pity the poor man who marries you, my dear."

The saucy smile returned. "I should be deeply wounded by those words, Lieutenant, but with that soft Virginia drawl you could say just anything. Now, tell me why you pity my future husband."

"Because, he'll never be able to let you out of his sight."

The dimples deepened. She leaned against him, standing on her toes. Her hands went around his neck, pulling him toward her as she whispered, "Why would he want to?"

"Good question."

Clark took the willing lips again, knowing that she had all the cards stacked in her favor. He would take only the liberties she allowed, and when she decided to cash in her chips, the game would be over. She had picked her time and place well. He wasn't fool enough to think he was anything more than her idea of a little adventure.

After a long leisurely kiss, she sank away from him with a trembling sigh. "I really must go back," she whispered.

He nodded. "I'll stay out here a few minutes, of course."

"Do be careful," she said, slipping away from him. In a moment she had gone inside and closed the door.

"Careful," he murmured, resting his head against the car behind him. "You, too." Someday that little minx was going to play with the wrong man. Or some poor fool would fall in love with her and not know it was hopeless. But not today.

Rebecca took her seat, noticing with pleasure that Aunt Belle had fallen asleep. Alicia, however, was wide-awake. "You were gone so long, I was worried," she whispered.

"There's a rail all around the platform. You would have to try to fall," Rebecca assured her in quiet tones.

"That's not what I meant." Alicia glanced furtively at her mother and lowered her voice until Rebecca could hardly hear it. "Was he a gentleman?"

Rebecca giggled and bit her lip. Nothing roused Aunt Belle's suspicion like merriment. "Barely," she whispered.

She knew Alicia was aware of her fondness for men. Alicia had come to her rescue a couple of times when Rebecca had nearly been caught sneaking in or out. Though Rebecca looked on the little flirtations and stolen kisses as innocent fun, Aunt Belle saw them as signs of loose character. Rebecca knew her father was treated to every detail in his sister's letters. At least every detail Belle knew or imagined. And that was part of the reason Rebecca hesitated to share too much of her escapades with her young cousin. What she didn't know, her mother couldn't force out of her.

Something else held her back, as well. This lieutenant was older than the others, more experienced. He had been a dangerous choice. She had a feeling that in another place he wouldn't have stopped with a kiss. The notion wasn't as alarming as it should have been.

Alicia was watching her expectantly. Rebecca grinned at her. "He pronounces prairie like it ends with *a*, and says the most charming things."

"Will you see him again?"

"Of course not." Rebecca heard more conviction in her voice than she felt.

"What if he insists?"

"Alicia," Rebecca hissed. "He won't insist. He's a gentleman."

"Barely."

Rebecca scowled at her cousin, wishing she'd be

quiet. She wanted to sit and savor the warmth that still tingled in her stomach. That was by far the best kiss ever. In fact, this was the first time she wanted to corner the same man a second time. She wondered if she *could* see him again. No, that was a bad idea. If they met under any other circumstances now, he might think she was a loose woman and expect more than a couple of kisses.

Too bad, she thought. He was incredibly charming.

When the train pulled into the station at Fort Riley, Clark was more than ready to get off. If he had to hear the dark-haired girl's voice or see the top of her head for much longer, he would be hustling her back out to the platform. He had no explanation for his reaction to her flirtation. It was the kind of thing he ran into often enough. On this trip back home, two different women had practiced their wiles on him. Neither had left him feeling confused the way this young lady had.

He got his bag and left the station, resisting the urge to see where the girl went. There were more important things to think about. At the post commander's headquarters, he dropped his bag beside the door and entered. Answering the orderly's salute, he requested a meeting with General Hale.

While the orderly stepped into the inner office, Clark took a look around the room. All headquarters looked much the same, dark and bare with only a few reflections of the person in charge. This is what my life has become, he thought, dark and bare. The observation had come to him once before, also after a visit home. Home? Virginia was hardly that anymore; he had been out here too long.

The orderly interrupted Clark's thoughts. "Please go in, Lieutenant," he said.

Clark nodded and entered the office. General Hale stood behind his desk, offering his hand and dismissing Clark's salute. "We've been expecting you. Welcome back to the West, Lieutenant," he said. "Did you have a pleasant trip home?"

"Yes, sir." Clark stood at ease as the general took his seat.

"I understand you've been at Fort Dodge and are to report to Fort Hays. You know they moved again?" He didn't wait for a response. "They were flooded out on the eighth. Moved farther west and closer to where the railroad will run. Colonel Huntington requested more men as well as supplies. These are due to leave…" he consulted a ledger on his desk "…in two days. I'm putting you in charge."

"Yes, sir."

"I believe you know Sergeant Whiting. He's been here working with the new recruits you'll be taking with you. He'll see about your quarters and anything else you need." The general's attention had already been drawn back to the papers on his desk. "Was there anything else?"

After the formalities of dismissal, Clark turned to leave the office. The orderly caught the door as he opened it, stepping aside and entering the inner office behind him. The door swung shut before Clark noticed three women waiting in the outer room. They all turned in his direction, but the dark-haired girl with the dimples was the only one he truly saw.

Habit let him walk past the orderly's desk toward the outside door. He managed a polite, "Ladies," as he passed. His hand was on the doorknob when the general burst from his office.

"Rebecca! This can't be little Becky Huntington! Why, dear child, you're all grown up!"

Clark managed to step outside and close the door gently behind him. He lifted his bag and stepped off the boardwalk with no real sense of what he was doing. *Rebecca Huntington? Colonel Huntington?* His daughter, no doubt. And he wasn't lucky enough for the general to be addressing the blond girl. He had heard the returned greeting and recognized the dark-haired girl's voice.

If the incident on the train became common knowledge, the good colonel would not look on it quite the way he did. And the little minx could be expected to protect herself above all else. He could find himself up to his bars in trouble.

* * *

In the headquarters building, Rebecca tried not to wonder about the lieutenant's purpose. She returned General Hale's greeting and introduced her traveling companions. "My aunt and cousin will be living with Father and me at Fort Hays," she explained. "I heard you were here and couldn't pass through Fort Riley without dropping in to see you."

"Myrtle will be overjoyed. You'll all stay with us, of course. Let me take you to the house. Masters, see about a carriage."

The orderly saluted smartly and left, and the general saw to chairs for the ladies. "How long will we have the pleasure of your company?"

Rebecca seated herself primly in the straight-backed chair before she answered. "Only until tomorrow. We'll be taking the train to the end of the track, then a coach on to Fort Hays."

"Oh, but my dear, the coaches have stopped!"

"Stopped?" croaked Belle. "How have they stopped?"

Hale leaned against the orderly's desk, crossing his feet at the ankles. "I don't mean to alarm you fair ladies, but there has been an uprising, and all the civilian coaches have stopped until the hostiles have been remanded to reservations."

"Indians?" Alicia and Belle said together, the former with more awe and less terror than the latter.

"I insist that you wait here," Hale continued, folding his arms. "The end of the track is Ellsworth.

We're not even running supplies through there yet. Last I heard they have but four completed buildings, three of which are saloons."

"But surely the army hasn't stopped moving," Rebecca said. Much as she liked General Hale and his wife, she didn't want to wait here. Ending the uprising could take all summer, and she wanted to see her father and get settled again. "When is the next supply caravan?"

"In two days. But that isn't fit transportation for gentlewomen like yourselves." Rebecca thought his smile was somewhat condescending. Before she could retort, he continued, "Your father didn't plan an escort of any kind? I'd like to, but..."

Rebecca sat forward. "Excuse me, General, but if there are Indians to be caught, I doubt if either of you can spare the men. No, the caravan will do." Rebecca didn't turn to see her companions' reactions to her pronouncement. The general's dubious smile was enough.

"Dear girl," he began, but the orderly chose that moment to return and announce their carriage was ready. General Hale ushered them out of the headquarters and helped them one by one into the carriage. He drove them personally to his quarters, a house near enough that Rebecca could easily have walked the distance in the time it had taken to hitch up the carriage.

Myrtle Hale greeted them effusively and her husband left, promising to send Masters to the train station for their trunks. Myrtle sent her maid scurrying to find places for them to sleep while she led them to a tiny, overdecorated room that served as a parlor. The room was dark; its one small window was covered with heavy drapes of faded maroon. But it was cooler than it had been outside.

"Please sit down," Myrtle directed. "I'll put water on for tea."

"Pardon me," Belle murmured. "If you'll direct me to the privy…"

"Of course. Make yourselves comfortable, girls."

The moment the older women were gone Alicia whispered, "That was your young lieutenant in the general's office."

Rebecca nodded, not wanting them to be overheard. She crossed the room to sit in an ornately carved chair.

Alicia followed. She picked up a china figure from the table next to Rebecca, but instead of inspecting it cast a furtive glance toward the door. Rebecca could see a faint circle where the figure had been. Now that she had seen it, she could smell the dust. Aunt Belle would be shocked but Rebecca knew how difficult it was to keep the dust out when the wind blew nearly all the time.

"But what's he doing here?" Alicia whispered.

Rebecca shrugged and tried to sound bored. "He's a soldier. This is a fort. He probably belongs here."

Why, in heaven's name, didn't I think of that? She let her fingers trace the carvings in the arm of the chair.

Alicia replaced the figure and was silent for a long moment. "I wish I could be like you," she sighed, sinking into a chair opposite Rebecca.

Rebecca raised a questioning eyebrow.

"The way you talk to men, I mean, and flirt." She giggled a little, and Rebecca imagined her remembering her bold perusal of the lieutenant on the train. She suppressed a groan. "If they even look at me," Alicia went on, "I turn suddenly stupid."

"Some men like that," Rebecca said.

Alicia smiled, a gentle, knowing smile that always caught Rebecca by surprise. "But I don't like the men that do."

"Do what?" Belle entered the parlor and looked around. She chose a large padded chair near the door and, as she settled into it, began fanning herself. "Is it always this hot?"

"It's a little unusual this early in the summer," Rebecca offered, hoping Aunt Belle would forget the comment she had overheard. "We get some lovely weather in September."

"This whole trip has been more misery than anything else," Belle muttered.

Rebecca bit her tongue. Father had told her once his sister felt things more sharply than others. Her own assessment was less charitable. Yet she tried to be patient. After all, both Belle and Alicia were in mourning.

Myrtle came with the tea tray, offering each a lovely china cup and saucer. "Just one cup, and I'll let you rest. You must all be exhausted from your trip. I find train travel so tedious."

Alicia and Belle groaned their agreement while Rebecca opened her mouth to disagree. Feeling outnumbered, she settled into the uncomfortable chair as best she could and listened to the others talk. When the maid announced that a room had been made ready where they could rest, the women rose. Rebecca expressed a desire to walk. The others eyed her with considerable surprise but didn't argue.

Alicia caught her arm and held her back as the older women left the room. "Are you going to look for your lieutenant?" she whispered.

"He's not *my* lieutenant," Rebecca hissed.

"What will you do if you meet him?"

"I'll…" Oh drat, what would she do? "Come with me," she suggested impulsively, taking her cousin's hand.

Alicia shrank away from her. "I can't now. I'm too tired. And what would Mother say?"

Rebecca let her go. She resigned herself to staying at the house. In the kitchen she washed her face, then filled a tall glass with water to take with her to the porch. There were no chairs so Rebecca sat on the top step and listened to the flag snap as she sipped her water.

The row of three officers' quarters faced another row across the parade ground. The barracks buildings made up the other two sides of the square. There was very little going on in this part of the fort this time of the day. She longed to visit the sutler's store, to walk past the blacksmith's shop, the saddler's, the carpenter's, to see if they had changed since her last visit. But she couldn't risk running into the lieutenant.

She leaned against the porch post and closed her eyes. Why should he have such an effect on her? All her other conquests had been easy to dismiss. She should dismiss him as well and take her walk. She had nearly resolved to do just that when she thought of coming face-to-face with him. Her pulse raced just imagining it. She would probably blush and stammer like Alicia.

She would have liked to examine her surprising reaction a bit more, but she saw the general approaching. She quickly rose and went to meet him. "I didn't expect you so soon, General."

"I managed to get away a little early. Are the others resting?"

"I believe so." Rebecca resumed her seat on the stairs and pulled the general down beside her. "Can't we really go with the supply train?"

"My dear, you're all welcome here until the

coaches are running again. It'll make a much more comfortable trip.''

Rebecca let her eyes do the pleading. "Every time we moved when I was young we would travel with the garrison. And don't tell me Aunt Belle isn't used to it. Mama wasn't either until her first trip.''

"But the uprising…''

"Indians virtually never attack large groups of soldiers unless cornered.'' A glance at Hale showed how little effect her words had. She cast her eyes downward. "It's been so long since I've seen Father.'' Why was it that whimpering worked better with men than logic?

"But—'' He hesitated.

Rebecca turned away and said in a small voice, "If it's impossible, I understand.'' That would have been the *coup de grace* with Father.

"Don't cry, dear. Are you so eager to leave us?''

Rebecca kept her dry eyes averted and shrugged her shoulders delicately.

"Well, now, I can see how it is. But I don't feel right ordering someone to take you. Perhaps you should talk to the officer I put in charge of the expedition. If he's agreeable, I'll let you go.''

Rebecca threw her arms around his neck. "Oh thank you, General,'' she said, keeping her voice soft and a trifle shaky as she slipped from his arms. "Who is he? I'll go talk to him now.''

"Name's Forrester. I believe he'll be camping near

the commissary building. He's likely very busy now. Perhaps you should wait until morning.''

"Yes, of course," Rebecca said. In the morning she could contrive to look less wilted.

"I better tell Myrtle I'm home. If I know her, she's busy with plans for an officer's ball to honor our guests. She'll be wanting my orderly to notify everyone."

Rebecca smiled and waved to him as he came to his feet and left her. She had plans of her own to make. This Forrester, whoever he was, would have trouble denying her request.

Shortly after breakfast, before the day had a chance to become miserably hot, Rebecca made her way toward the commissary. She had put on one of her most flattering dresses, not at all suitable for travel but exactly what she needed to convince Forrester that he wanted three women with his supply caravan. Every soldier she met offered directions. She gave them each a grateful smile, though she was well aware of where she was going.

She saw the tent from a considerable distance. As she confidently approached it she noticed the officer, bent over a field desk. Alerted perhaps by a chorus of "mornin', ma'am," the officer came to his feet. The clean-shaven jaw beneath the shadow of the campaign hat belonged to her lieutenant from the train.

What incredibly rotten luck. Her footsteps faltered

as she felt a strong desire to turn back. Pride kept her moving toward the lieutenant and put her brightest smile on her lips. "So *you're* Lieutenant Forrester?"

He doffed his hat, placing it under his arm, and stood almost at attention. "At your service, Miss Huntington."

Rebecca bit her lip as she watched him. He was cool and formal; the softly accented voice wasn't nearly as charming now that it lacked its former warmth. A quick glance told her there was no one close enough to overhear. Still she kept her voice low. "I came to talk about leaving with the supply wagons tomorrow, but perhaps we should talk about what happened on the train."

"What happened on the train, ma'am? I dallied with the colonel's daughter. I am aware that I could find myself accused of conduct unbecoming an officer. Are you here to make a deal?"

Rebecca knew her eyes had widened and her mouth was nearly hanging open. She surely looked like an idiot, but she couldn't help it. "Oh dear," she murmured. After a deep shaky breath, she managed a tiny smile. "I was hoping to persuade you not to think too badly of me, but I can see I'm too late."

She had counted on her words softening him, but they seemed to have no effect. His face was as unmoving as his taut body. She gave up all efforts at smiling and whispered, "I'm not a loose woman, Lieutenant."

"I know that."

His words offered small comfort. Her hands were shaking, a most unwanted reaction to this man, and she clutched them firmly behind her back. "I just wanted you to kiss me."

"And I did." He paused for a moment, and she thought she finally saw a flicker of warmth in his gray eyes. "But it won't happen again."

"Pity." Rebecca knew it was not the ladylike thing to say, but it was the God's truth. She felt a wave of relief when he gave her a slight nod in agreement.

"That it is," he whispered.

Rebecca gazed at the handsome face, wishing he would smile. His pale eyes, full lips and wonderful jaw brought back very pleasant memories. She shook herself, remembering her errand. "I came to ask if my companions and I could travel with the wagons tomorrow."

"Do I have a choice, ma'am?"

"If I say yes, will you think better of me?" She smiled her brightest smile and watched for a reaction.

"Perhaps," he said, as cool as ever.

"Enough that you'll agree to let us go?" Her smile was beginning to falter. With his next words, it died completely.

"That's doubtful."

His oh-so-military bearing and polite-but-cold responses were beginning to wear on Rebecca's patience. She felt herself close to losing her temper, a big mistake, she knew. She took another deep breath and tried not to grit her teeth. "I'm sure I can convince the general to order you to take us along."

"I'm aware of that, Miss Huntington."

They stared at each other for a long moment. It took all Rebecca's resolve to keep from turning away. She broke the standoff with a question she hoped would be appeasing. "What is your main objection to our going?"

"The civilian coaches have stopped for a reason, ma'am. It would be far safer for you to remain here until the problem has been dealt with."

"But they haven't attacked soldiers."

"Not yet, ma'am, but three women along might be all the added temptation they need. I understand they've already taken hostages."

Rebecca considered his words. She certainly didn't want to put the soldiers in more danger by her presence. With a sigh, she said, "I'll discuss it with the general," and turned to go.

"I'm sure you will."

She didn't acknowledge his last words.

Clark stood until the swaying bustle had disappeared then sat, staring at the papers in front of him. He had to reconcile himself to the flirt's presence on the caravan. He hadn't been honest with her; it wasn't the Indians he was worried about. It was the trouble she would cause among the troops. She wasn't the type of woman any man found easy to ignore.

Chapter Two

Rebecca felt like dancing. And of course that was exactly what she would be doing soon, though probably not with the handsome young lieutenant.

After she had left him early that morning, she had gone to General Hale's office. She had said the lieutenant was reluctant to take them, skirting the fact that he had flatly refused. She had suggested a word from the general about her lifelong experience with the army might allay his fears. A mention of her devotion to her father. An allusion to the need of her grieving aunt and cousin to be settled in a loving home.

The general didn't bite.

Next she had gone home, hoping to enlist the help of Aunt Belle, but found her in the midst of planning a ball with Myrtle and incapable of worrying about anything else. In fact, she suspected that the older woman wasn't particularly excited about venturing into what she called the wilderness.

Shortly before Hale was expected home for lunch, Rebecca had found an onion in the kitchen, rubbed her fingertips against its sliced side, and waited for the general on the porch steps.

Where logic had failed, tears won. The general assured her he would order the lieutenant to take them and make an ambulance available for their use. The afternoon had been devoted to altering some clothes with Alicia as her skilled, though doubtful assistant.

Now Rebecca sat in the Hale kitchen while Alicia pulled her dark thick tresses into a fashionable coil. With the bulk of it pinned in place and decorated with a carved alabaster comb, Alicia turned to retrieve the curling iron from the stove. Rebecca had already fixed her cousin's hair and fat blond ringlets caressed the curve of her bare shoulder and neck.

"Every man at the dance will want to touch those curls," Rebecca said.

Alicia gave her a shy smile. "You did a wonderful job, Rebecca."

"I wasn't complimenting my work, I was complimenting the way you look."

Alicia shrugged. "Hold still. I don't want to burn you."

With great care, Alicia turned the wisps of hair around Rebecca's face to tiny curls, then nodded her satisfaction. "Now all we have to do is wait for Mother."

"I don't think Mrs. Hale will allow her to dawdle much longer," Rebecca said. "She's certain the dance won't start without her, and she may be right."

"Let's wait in the parlor," Alicia suggested. "It's so warm in here we're liable to wilt. We want the curls to last until the fourth dance."

"Ah, yes," Rebecca agreed, slipping her arm through Alicia's and leaving the kitchen with her. "And anyone who is still in perfect order by the fourth dance hasn't been dancing and will remain a wallflower the rest of the night."

Alicia sighed dramatically. "Do you know how often I've had to run out during the fourth dance to splash a little water in my face and tug at my curls?"

Rebecca shook her head. "Never, I'd wager, unless you were turning the poor boys away. Have you looked at yourself in the mirror, cousin? You're beautiful!"

To Rebecca's frustration Alicia shook her head, the pink blush that came to her cheeks making her all the more appealing. "I'm serious, Alicia. You could have all the men falling at your feet with the least bit of flirting. It works for me, and I'm too tall and too skinny and my hair's impossibly ordinary."

"And those dimples in your cheeks are just horrid, too."

Rebecca grinned. "So I have one overworked asset. Men give you more attention than you want, and I have to work so hard to get any." She gave an exaggerated and unconvincing sigh.

"I saw how hard you worked on the lieutenant. One smile and he would have followed you...well, he *did* follow you."

"I know I shouldn't do it," Rebecca said, feeling unrepentant in spite of her words. "But they are so nice to touch and...kiss."

"They? Men in general? Don't you believe in love?"

"Oh, Lord, I hope not!"

Alicia gave a startled laugh. "Rebecca! All women want to fall in love."

Rebecca shook her head. "Not me. I think it's wonderful fun to...to...dazzle a man. It'd be hard to do that with a husband around."

Alicia looked truly shocked. "You're awful!"

They heard footsteps on the stairs and knew the others were finally ready. Rebecca leaned close to Alicia and whispered. "True. And I'm willing to teach you everything I know."

They had to take a carriage to the dance so the ladies wouldn't ruin their slippers on the way. Alicia was almost giddy, and Rebecca guessed she was torn between wanting to flirt with the men and wanting to hide behind a potted plant. The girl really was shy.

"This is just lovely," Myrtle said for the fifth time. "We get so few guests."

"The hall was decorated this afternoon," Hale said. "My wife called in an entire troop of officers' wives."

Myrtle nudged her husband with her elbow. "Don't you dare make any remark about them being at my command. They all volunteered to help when I told them about our guests."

The moment the general entered the hall a small band struck up a waltz. Hale escorted his wife to the center of the floor. Myrtle smiled regally as her husband danced her around the room, and in a few minutes a few others joined them on the floor.

"You'd think she was the queen," Alicia whispered.

"In this society, she is," Rebecca answered.

"And *you* will be when you get to Hays. The commanding officer's daughter."

Rebecca moved her cousin away from the door to a spot where they could better watch the crowd. "I hadn't thought of that," she said. Her eyes scanned the faces, looking for a particular lieutenant.

"The social leader," Alicia added near her ear. "The standard for propriety."

"I think I'll abdicate."

"There he is."

"Who?" Rebecca asked innocently, though her eyes had fallen on Forrester at the moment her cousin had spoken.

"Your lieutenant. Will he ask you to dance?"

"I doubt it. If he does, he'll probably step on my toes—on purpose."

Before Alicia could reply she was claimed by a young officer. Rebecca smiled as her cousin was whirled away. Soon she was asked as well. After three dances with six different partners, she pleaded exhaustion and sought out the refreshment table.

After a moment Alicia joined her. "I believe I'm adequately wilted, don't you?"

"In the loveliest sense," Rebecca said. "Are you having fun?"

Alicia nodded, sipping her punch daintily. "I haven't dazzled anyone, though."

Rebecca was about to answer when a decidedly wilted Aunt Belle huffed up beside them. "I'm nearly done in. I'm sure I shouldn't dance, but Mrs. Hale said it would be cruel not to, there being so few women. How are you girls faring?"

"Quite well, Aunt Belle," Rebecca answered. "Aren't the decorations lovely?"

When Belle turned to look around her, Rebecca tipped her head at Alicia indicating her desire to move father from the refreshments.

"They look like leftover Independence Day banners."

"Yes, I suppose," Rebecca agreed with a grin. "But they go so well with the gold buttons, don't you think?"

Beside her Alicia muffled a giggle. Aunt Belle

didn't seem amused. "They're brass," she said, pointedly.

Rebecca looked out across the room, taking in the host of blue uniforms, buttons, bars, and braid. "It's all in how you look at it," she murmured. "Oh, Aunt Belle, you look absolutely drained. You had better get some punch."

"Yes, I suppose."

As soon as the older woman turned away, Rebecca steered her cousin toward an unoccupied corner, leaning close to whisper, "Who would you like to dazzle?"

"Besides your young lieutenant?"

Rebecca glanced up and caught him watching her. She had been at least half aware of where he was all evening. Alicia noticed the slip and the gleam in her blue eyes was positively wicked. Rebecca was almost tempted to turn her loose on him, just to show her she wouldn't be jealous. Almost. Considering it made her want to grit her teeth. Lord, she *would* be jealous! Hoping to hide her feelings from her cousin she said lightly, "We better leave him alone. He's been dazzled recently. It's a little like being burned."

"That's awful, Rebecca. I don't want to hurt anyone."

Rebecca shushed her cousin, looking quickly around to be sure they hadn't been overheard. "I didn't hurt him," she whispered emphatically. "He's just not thrilled that we're going with him tomorrow, and he thinks I'd use the...uh...encounter on the train against him if he refused."

"But wouldn't that reflect as badly on you as him?"

"Not the way he thinks I'd tell it. Oh, Alicia it gets complicated. Take my word, and pick out somebody else."

While Alicia was making her choice, Rebecca glanced again in Forrester's direction. Lord, he was still watching her!

"That one," Alicia whispered, "with the mustache."

"Ah, a colonel! Very good, Alicia! Now, you need to watch him until he looks in your direction. Make eye contact, then give him a smile."

"All right," Alicia whispered. "But don't you look at him at all, or he'll ask you to dance instead."

"I'll plead exhaustion and push you into his arms."

Clark couldn't hear what the ladies were saying, but they had been whispering together for quite some time, and Miss Huntington had glanced in his direction more than once. He hoped he made her nervous, but he seriously doubted it.

He wanted to dance with her. It was ridiculous, but true. He wanted to feel her warm body move against his again. He wanted to know if she had given in to convention and worn a corset. And he hated to think that half a dozen other men already knew.

He realized he had actually started toward her and tried to stop himself. Instead, he thought of excuses for asking her to dance. They would be traveling together; they should be on friendly terms. He didn't want her imagining that he was afraid of her. He didn't want to pass up a chance to touch her.

He had made his way across two-thirds of the room when he noticed another man doing the same. The minx seemed to have set her sights on a colonel. Well, why was he surprised? The room probably looked like a huge buffet to her. He had only imagined her glances in his direction.

He stopped and waited for the colonel to claim her. He would dance one dance with the blonde, then leave. He hadn't wanted to come in the first place. To his surprise, when the colonel moved onto the dance floor, it was the blonde he had on his arm. Miss Huntington was standing alone, holding two cups and smiling after them like a proud mother.

He moved quickly to her side. "Your cousin's a fast learner," he said.

She wasn't surprised to see him, but the comment had taken her off guard. She gave herself a moment then smiled up at him. "Why, whatever do you mean?"

The little tease was mimicking his accent. He would ignore it. "You were instructing her in the fine art of flirting, weren't you? It's probably quite a challenge teaching someone something that comes so naturally to you.''

Her dimples deepened. ''I do my best. Oh, look, here comes General Hale.''

Her means of escape, if that was what she wanted. And his, too. But he didn't want to escape.

Rebecca spoke to the general before he came to a complete stop beside her. ''General, your wife has given such a lovely party. We're having a wonderful time.''

''I'm glad you're enjoying it, my dear. Lieutenant.''

Clark returned the greeting. He should excuse himself. He would. At the moment he opened his mouth, he felt her hand come down lightly on his arm. The cups were stacked in her other hand, and her attention was on the general. He looked down at the hand to make sure he hadn't imagined it.

''General, could you do me a favor?''

What trouble did the lady have in mind?

''Anything, my dear,'' the general said gallantly. Clark wanted to groan.

''Take care of our cups, will you? The lieutenant has just asked me to dance.''

It happened so quickly he felt a little light-headed. One moment he was ready to face General Hale's displeasure, the next the dark-haired beauty was in his arms. After a moment he said, ''I don't recall asking you to dance.''

"But you did!" she declared, the picture of innocence. He opened his mouth to disagree only to have her add, "Your eyes did, at any rate."

"I suppose I'll have to take your word for it."

She smiled up at him, her eyes dancing. "I'll admit I might have seen what I wanted to. But if I hadn't claimed this dance, you and the general would have started talking about army business, and I would have been bored to death with no graceful way of escape. No one's asked me to dance for just ages."

"Two dances." At her surprised look he clarified, "You haven't danced for two dances."

"Keeping track, Lieutenant?"

Clark sighed and held her closer, spinning her around, hoping to distract her. The best policy for dealing with this young lady was to keep his mouth shut. She seemed content to dance, probably savoring her victory. He decided to savor the sensation of her in his arms. He wasn't sure if he was relieved or disappointed to feel the stays of a corset under the fabric of her dress.

She sighed gently; he felt it more than heard it. Probably calculated seduction. He would hate for her to know how well it was working. He wanted to hustle her outside to some lonely spot and claim at least a kiss. He didn't dare. And she knew it.

Her right hand in his left shifted slightly. It felt like a caress, though it was probably calculated as well. They had begun the dance with their hands in the normal position, but now her fingers were wrapped around his thumb. It made her hand look small, vulnerable. A dangerous illusion, he decided.

When the music stopped, they broke away to join in the smattering of applause. He was torn between his desire to ask for another dance and his conviction that his only chance of leaving with a shred of dignity was to leave at once.

"Thank you, Miss Huntington. It's been a pleasure."

"Does it have to end so soon? There doesn't seem to be a line of partners waiting for their turns."

"Spread that smile around, and there will be. Good night, ma'am."

Rebecca watched him go. She couldn't believe she had flirted with him. Of course, it was almost automatic. But he already thought so poorly of her she should have left him alone. And he hadn't responded at all!

Someone tapped her shoulder. "Would you care to dance?"

She shook her head, waving him away with barely a glance, her attention still on the door through which the lieutenant had gone. How could he be so immune to her when he did such wonderful things to her senses? Her heart was still racing, her fingers were tingling. No doubt, her cheeks were flushed, perhaps even feverish. And he casually walked away.

After a gentlemanly compliment, true, but still he

found her easy to resist. In fact, he had barely talked to her. She felt a smile tug at her lips and let it spread across her face. He had barely talked *after* he admitted to watching her all evening.

Clark sat behind the field desk, fighting the wind as he went through the last of the figures Sergeant Whiting had provided. The train was due to leave in one hour, but he had a feeling they would be delayed waiting for the women in whatever accommodation General Hale had deemed appropriate. As ordered.

He heard unhurried footsteps and caught a glimpse of uniformed legs on the other side of his desk. "One moment, soldier," he said, marking his place and placing a rock on the stack of papers. He looked up at his visitor. And leaped to his feet, sending his chair crashing to the ground behind him.

"Miss Huntington?" It was a stupid question. Of course it was Miss Huntington. But she was dressed in a cavalry private's uniform. He supposed he should be glad she hadn't decided to outrank him. Her glossy black hair was pulled tightly back from her face and tucked precariously under a broad-brimmed hat. Her eyes were brown sparkles and her cheeks were deeply dimpled.

"Am I less temptation now, sir?"

"What?" Clark's power of reasoning seemed to have fled with his breath.

"You said three women might be temptation for the Indians. Now we look like three more soldiers."

Clark shook his head. "Ma'am, you don't look like a soldier." He was trying hard to keep his eyes on her face and off the shapely body that filled out the uniform blouse and pants in a most unusual way.

"Well, not up close."

She sounded exasperated, and he tried to pull himself together. An official question seemed to be the best way. "How soon will you be ready to travel?"

She brought her heels together. "Ready now! Sir!" This was followed by a smart salute. His hand moved to answer it before he caught himself. He had the distinct impression he was being mocked.

"We leave in one hour. Soldier."

She answered his sarcasm with a dimpled grin, turned on her heel and marched away. She had disappeared from view before he realized he was grinning.

Rebecca stuffed her hair under her hat for at least the fourth time that morning. She had expected to have a little trouble with the wind, but Aunt Belle had refused to let her roll up the canvas sides of the ambulance more than a couple of inches for fear someone would see them in their scandalous outfits. As a result, there was barely a breath of air.

And it wasn't the shaking wagon that caused the problem either; it was her hair. It was too thick and too long and impossible to keep in place. She should have chosen a hat three sizes bigger. The picture she would present with a huge hat perched atop her head made her chuckle.

"What you can find to laugh about is beyond me," muttered Aunt Belle.

A bench had been fashioned along one side of the wagon and padded with bedding for the ladies' comfort. Aunt Belle wasn't impressed. She had been sullen all morning.

"Things aren't as bad as all that." Rebecca patted her aunt's blue-clad knee hoping to improve her temper. "We have more space than we would in a stagecoach, and we have it all to ourselves. Besides, at a stage stop we would only get a moment's rest while they changed the teams. This way we'll have more opportunity to walk about as the teams are rested."

"It'll take us longer to get there, then," was Belle's reply.

Rebecca resisted the urge to roll her eyes. "Not as long as it would take if we waited out this war," she said, forgetting for a moment that she was trying to soothe her aunt.

Aunt Belle shuddered.

"Come over here, Mother, and watch the prairie go by," Alicia suggested. She had abandoned the seat an hour ago and had curled up on a bedroll where she could peek through the small opening between the wooden box and canvas side.

"There's nothing out there to see," Aunt Belle declared.

"There are the soldiers," Rebecca said, winking at Alicia.

Aunt Belle nearly came out of her seat. "Alicia! Come away from there before they see you!"

"They already know we're here," Rebecca reasoned. "Besides, it's just a crack. What will they see?"

"It's unseemly!"

Alicia rose obediently. She was short enough to stand upright under the square frame that held the canvas. Rebecca mouthed a "sorry" as her cousin passed to take a seat on the other side of Belle.

Alicia gave her a forgiving smile. "Will we be stopping for lunch, do you think?"

"Of course," Rebecca assured her. "I'll ask the driver if he knows anything." Before her aunt could stop her, she flung herself toward the front of the wagon and scrambled under the canvas and over the back of the seat.

"Mind if I join you for a few minutes?" she asked the driver after he had hastily made room for her. "It's much cooler out here than inside."

"I can stop and help you roll up the sides if you'd like," he offered.

"That's kind of you," she said, trying to locate the lieutenant in the column ahead. "Aunt Belle prefers her privacy. Your name is Brooks, isn't it?" He had been introduced that morning when he was assigned to drive their wagon, but she had barely noticed the young enlisted man.

"Yes, ma'am. Victor Brooks."

"Have you heard when we'll be stopping to rest?" The new recruits were riding four abreast directly in front of their wagon. She stood up for a moment to get a better view beyond, assuming the lieutenant was leading the column.

"Ain't been in the army long enough to even make a guess. All I know is to mind my sergeant, steer clear of officers, and eat whenever they give me a chance."

Rebecca laughed. "I hope they give us that chance soon."

"Me and my messmates are supposed to cook for you ladies as well as ourselves. I reckon that means we roast your rabbit before we boil our salt pork."

Rebecca turned and studied the soldier for the first time. Judging by his smooth skin, he was in his early twenties, but there was a hardness about his eyes that made him look older. She couldn't tell if he was resentful of the assignment or had intended his comment as a joke.

"Oh dear," she said with a sigh. "I seem to have forgotten to set out my rabbit traps so tonight you'll probably be cooking double rations of pork."

Brooks gave a mirthless laugh. "Not likely, ma'am. Dixie Boy will be looking out for himself, and for you too, I reckon. I imagine there's a hunting party out what won't get a bite of what they kill.''

Dixie Boy? She had a feeling this soldier was headed for trouble. Arguing with him wouldn't help, though, especially if he turned out to be right. He had evidently heard stories, she had too, of officers who dined in elegance while the troops ate the standard rations. Or substandard as they called them.

"Did you see a hunting party go?"

"Three men were sent ahead a while ago."

Rebecca scowled. Why would she be so disappointed if Brooks was right? "Maybe they're scouting out a river crossing," she suggested.

"I wouldn't know, ma'am."

"Tell you what, soldier," Rebecca said, standing again as the column ahead mounted a rise. "If you turn out to be right, I'll see you get a share."

"Why, that's kind of you, ma'am," Brooks said.

Rebecca smiled. She had located him finally, riding a bay horse in the lead of the column. She sat down when he was once again hidden by the other soldiers. "But that won't be till evening anyway. The noon meal is usually too hurried to cook anything. And General Hale's wife packed us a lunch."

"I should have guessed."

She leaned closer and spoke softly. "If it won't make your messmates jealous, I'll see if I can't save something back."

"What my messmates don't know, can't upset 'em."

They caught up with the three outriders at a creek and rested just beyond it. Stock was fed and watered, fires were quickly built and coffee boiled. Rebecca wanted to spread a blanket on the ground and eat Mrs. Hale's lunch picnic style, but Aunt Belle refused to leave the wagon except for a brief excursion into the trees. Even with Rebecca and Alicia standing guard, she found the experience humiliating.

Brooks offered them coffee, but otherwise they were left alone to eat their lunch in the same confining space they had shared all morning. Rebecca listened to the voices of the men outside and felt like a prisoner. She hoped the lieutenant would come to check on their well-being and comfort but knew Aunt Belle would probably voice her complaints. When he hadn't come by the time they started down the trail, she told herself it was just as well.

She slipped out to the seat again shortly after they started, bringing the driver two pieces of cold chicken. He seemed surprised, though not particularly pleased to receive the offering, as if he would rather have had his worst notions confirmed than have the chicken to eat. She decided she didn't like Victor Brooks.

Still, she determined to be nice to him. She and her companions were dependent on him in many respects, and he would no doubt take more care for their comfort if she was kind to him.

Brooks, busily eating the chicken, didn't seem inclined to talk so Rebecca watched the column ahead, especially the officer when she could get a glimpse of him, and wished she was riding alongside him. As she imagined smiling up at him, the wind took a swipe at her hat. She grabbed for it too late.

"Stop!"

Brooks stared at her. Only after seeing the heat in his eyes did she realize that her hair had come completely unpinned and tumbled around her shoulders.

She gathered it into her fist, and Brooks came to his senses, hauling on the reins. He jumped from the wagon and Rebecca leaned around the side to see if the next team had already trampled her hat. The freight wagons were still a few yards behind, and Brooks sprinted to her hat, bringing it back to her at a run. He was in the seat and calling to the team before the next wagon was forced out of line.

"Thanks," Rebecca said, brushing at the dust on the hat.

"My pleasure, ma'am."

Rebecca frowned. She would have to go back inside the wagon and try again to pin up her hair. She probably ought to stay there. Aunt Belle didn't approve of her spending time with the driver. Of course, Aunt Belle didn't approve of anything.

Still, until she found a way to keep her hat in place,

she would have to stay inside. Stopping the ambulance to retrieve it would be considered a nuisance by a certain officer in charge.

That evening, Clark set up the field desk and took out his journal. He had written half a page when a uniformed figure approached his desk. His first reaction was to finish the sentence. Then he remembered his experience of the morning. He looked up and came instantly to his feet, barely avoiding knocking over his chair again.

"Ma'am. This will take some getting used to." Her hat was in her hand and her dark hair was loose around her shoulders. He was sure he had never seen a woman's hair like that outside the bedroom. He shook off the image.

"Not for me." She gave him a conspiratorial grin that nearly disarmed him. "All this time I thought women were clumsy, but we hobble ourselves with our dresses."

Clark had no response for that. Feeling like a fool as he did every time she was nearby, he escaped behind his military training. "Is there something I can do for you, ma'am?"

"I have a problem," she said, but she didn't look particularly concerned.

"What's his name?"

The girl looked positively hurt. He almost regretted his bluntness, but it had been a reasonable guess.

"Not that kind of problem. Aunt Belle took my scissors."

Scissors? "Would you like her arrested, ma'am?"

She shot him a grin that told him she liked the idea. "No, I don't want her arrested. I wanted to know if you have a pair I can borrow."

"Sorry, ma'am."

"A knife?" she asked.

He drew a large bowie knife out of a sheath at his waist, certain the size would change her mind. "May I ask what you need it for?"

She looked from the knife to his face and grinned. "I'm having trouble keeping my hat on over all this hair. Would you do the honors?" She spun around, tossing her hair over her shoulders. It cascaded down her back in dark, shimmering waves.

Clark stared. "Ma'am?"

She turned to face him, sighing in exasperation. "I want you to cut my hair." She paused, but he was speechless. "I can't pass as a soldier like this, can I?"

"Ma'am," he pleaded, making a mental note to thank Mrs. Evans for hiding her scissors. "I could never explain this to your father."

"Lieutenant, we are probably being watched or will be as we travel farther west. You said yourself that women might tempt the hostiles to attack. With this much hair showing, I am plainly a woman."

"Or an Indian scout," he interjected hopefully.

She chose to ignore him. "If I don't keep my hat on I'm going to be sunburned. I could die of sunstroke. Do you want to explain *that* to my father?" She paused a moment, to give him time to digest her comment, he supposed, then turned her back again. "Slice it off at about my shoulders."

"Perhaps you could stay in the wagon." Even as he said it he knew that would be too much to ask of someone like Rebecca.

She spun around. "With Aunt Belle? All day, every day? For a week? I'll go mad. Wouldn't you?"

She turned her back on him again. When he made no move toward her, she tossed, "Lieutenant," over her shoulder. There was just enough threat in her voice to irritate him. He stepped around the desk and took the dark tresses in his left hand. She deserved this, he thought. Let *her* explain it to her father.

His knife was sharp, and it took only a moment. When the final cut was made she tossed her head, turning the bluntly cut locks into curls. Placing the hat firmly on her head she sent him a grin. "Thanks," she said as she walked away.

Clark looked after her, down at the knife and handful of dark, soft hair, and back at the retreating figure. He realized with a start that his hands were shaking and his breathing had become labored. He returned the knife to its sheath but stared at the hair for a long moment while the wind tried to pull it from his grasp.

He had the fleeting feeling that he had just scalped her.

He drew a white handkerchief from his pocket and, entering his tent, spread it on his bunk. Carefully, not wanting to miss a strand, he placed his treasure on top and folded the handkerchief around it, tying it with a string from his pack. Then he unbuttoned his blouse and, without pausing to analyze his actions, tucked the bundle into the pocket in the lining, next to his heart.

Chapter Three

Aunt Belle would probably swoon. Then she would try to find a way to punish her. But Aunt Belle's authority had diminished with every mile they put between themselves and Chicago. Soon Rebecca would be back in her father's care, and he was easily managed.

Rebecca made her way from Lieutenant Forrester's tent to the ambulance, putting Aunt Belle out of her mind. The lieutenant's face was much more fun to think about. He tried so hard not to register any reaction that it took something outlandish, like a request that he cut her hair, to get him to so much as raise an eyebrow. Disconcerting him was worth anything Aunt Belle could think to do to her.

Alicia had set up a camp table and two chairs beside the ambulance and sat hunched over a book. She looked up when Rebecca arrived. "You actually did it," she whispered.

Rebecca took off her hat and gave her bobbed hair a toss. "Do you think you can get my scissors from your mother and trim it for me? I doubt if it's very even. Maybe you could cut it in layers, like a man's, so it'll lie better."

Alicia merely stared.

"Relax, Alicia." Rebecca moved to the other chair and put the hat on the ground beside her. She looked at the table for the first time. It was set with Aunt Belle's everyday china and flatware—probably this was her idea of practical. There were only two places and an extra plate sat atop Alicia's.

"Is Aunt Belle feeling all right?" She hoped her determination to cut her hair hadn't actually made her aunt ill.

"She won't come out," Alicia whispered.

Rebecca glanced at the wagon, noticing that the canvas had been unrolled completely. "Even now? There's nobody around."

"There's lots of men around." Alicia waved her hand to encompass the whole camp with its many little campfires. "Besides, our driver said he would be bringing our dinner soon. Mother doesn't want anybody to see her in the pants."

"She might as well change into a dress if she's never coming out of the wagon. Of course, then she would have no reason to *stay* in the wagon."

Alicia started to giggle, then touched her finger to her lips. "She's sure she will be instantly scalped."

"That's ridiculous. She'd be perfectly safe."

Alicia gaped at her a moment, then hissed, "You said women would attract the Indians. That's why we're wearing these awful pants."

Rebecca shook her head. "Lieutenant Forrester said that. I called his bluff."

"What!" Alicia clapped her hand over her mouth.

"There may be some truth in it," Rebecca acknowledged, "especially when we get farther west. Alicia, that wasn't the real reason he didn't want us along, but it was the reason he gave. The pants prevent him from claiming we disregarded his concerns."

Alicia leaned back and stared at Rebecca as if the explanation was too much to fathom. After nearly a full minute she asked, "What do you think was the real reason?"

Rebecca grinned. "He thinks I'll flirt with all the soldiers."

Alicia arched a brow. "And won't you?"

"No!" She tried to look indignant, but in the face of Alicia's knowing nod it was impossible. She grinned instead. "At least not until I get tired of Lieutenant Forrester."

Clark signaled a halt when he saw the rider. Sergeant Whiting relayed the order then squinted at the approaching figure. "He's riding a mule."

Clark lifted the binoculars that hung from his sad-

dle and took a look. "Some old-timer." He passed
the glasses to Whiting.

"I think it's Decker," Whiting said. "He's done
some scouting for the army."

"Hold the column. I'll see what he wants." He
spurred his horse forward.

"First Lieutenant Clark Forrester, Seventh Cavalry," he said when they had drawn rein near each
other.

"How do, Lieutenant?" The man extended his
hand. "Name's Carl Decker. Saw your dust from
over yonder. Soon as I knew you wasn't a band a
renegades, I decided I'd come on in, see if I could
share a fire and have some company for the night.
Startin' to get a little spooked out here alone."

"Sure thing, Mr. Decker." Clark turned his mount,
and they started back toward the waiting column.

"Don't nobody I know call me Mr. Decker. Carl,
maybe, or more likely Short Deck. On account a me
being not so tall, I reckon."

Clark shook his head. "They wouldn't call you
Short Deck because you cheat at cards, would they?"

Decker spat a stream of tobacco juice on the far
side of his mule. "Maybe," he said with a chuckle.

Clark waved the troops forward, and he and
Decker fell in alongside the sergeant.

"Short Deck," Whiting said. "I thought that was
you. Where you headed?"

"Hell, I don't know, Sam," the old man answered.

"I'm thinkin' about leavin' the state. Or I may just find myself a place to hole up over here in Salina or yonder in Abilene."

"I can imagine the accommodations you're looking for," Whiting said.

Decker laughed. "How far am I gonna be backtrackin' here, Lieutenant?"

"I planned to camp about a mile farther west."

"Don't mind trading a couple miles for some company. How many men ya got here?"

It was Whiting that answered. "Forty. Most of them green as grass."

"They'll do," Clark said, knowing at least a few of the men in question had heard their sergeant.

"Replacements for Hard Ass?"

"Most likely." Clark bit back a grin at one of several nicknames for Custer. The man had reached the rank of Brevet General during the war. He enjoyed the use of the title, though the reorganized army considered him a Lieutenant Colonel.

Decker added, "The boy general has more than his share of desertions, don't he?" He leaned over and spat tobacco juice on the ground. "Bull's-eye."

Clark didn't turn to see what the man had been aiming at. As he listened to his sergeant and their guest talk he hoped Decker didn't change his mind about heading east; if the man stayed with the column long enough Clark might have his own problem with deserters.

After supper, several of the troopers settled in near Clark's camp, curious about the stranger. Miss Huntington was one of them. He sensed her presence before he caught a glimpse of her. He ignored her, or tried to, not wanting to draw her to Decker's attention.

"You told us where you were going, Deck," Whiting said. "Tell us where you've been."

Decker sat Indian-style, his coffee cup in his hands. "I been down around Fort Larned with Hancock so I guess you can say I was there when this damn war started."

Clark couldn't pass up an opportunity to get more information than was in the official reports, even if it meant some green troopers would hear it as well. "What happened?"

"Well, there'd been some trouble, mostly with the Dog Soldiers, so Hancock comes down there. Sends for the chiefs. This was back in April, and we get a snowstorm. Chiefs have a time gettin' in. Hancock don't want to set back the deadline. He's gonna teach them a lesson if they're late.

"Well, they show up the evening of the deadline. Ol' Hancock decides to start the council immediately. What does he care if there's no sun to bless the proceedin's? He's not there to listen, anyhow. He's there to threaten. He insults those chiefs from here to Sunday. Insists the Cheyenne ain't actin' in good faith since Roman Nose ain't along." Decker shook his head at the memory.

"Roman Nose is Northern Cheyenne," Whiting put in.

Decker nodded. "Been livin' down here, though. Kinda a rabble-rouser. At best he'd be called a war chief. They send their peace chiefs to councils. Anyhow, the Indians went away mad.

"Day or so later Hancock takes his forces and heads for Red Arm Creek where the Cheyenne are camped. I'm along as scout, you understand. The Cheyenne fire the prairie, forcing us to camp away from the village. There's a standoff for a couple a days. When we surround the village we find it deserted."

"Of course it was." The feminine voice brought Clark's head up, and Decker's as well. "Hadn't Hancock ever heard of Sand Creek?"

She had crept closer during the narrative and sat only a few feet from him. As surprised as he was to find she had gotten so close without his notice, he was more surprised by the question. He hadn't expected the colonel's daughter to know anything about the '64 massacre, let alone connect the Colorado Volunteers' burning of that peaceful Cheyenne village with the Cheyenne's behavior now. Most people didn't seem to believe Indians had memories.

The troopers, however were more interested in the

woman than in the question. They were watching her more closely than they watched their guest.

Decker was clearly startled. Clark could guess what he was thinking. An effeminate boy? A woman in disguise that only he had seen through? Clark decided to let him wonder. Besides, she had asked a good question.

Decker recovered quickly, though he cast Whiting a questioning glance. "As a matter of fact, that's just what Roman Nose asked him. He came to parley during the standoff."

"What happened to the deserted village?" Clark asked, though he could guess.

With a flick of his wrist, Decker tossed his cold coffee on the ground, in lieu of tobacco juice, Clark supposed. "Hancock sends Custer after 'em, waits four days, and burns the village. Two hundred fifty lodges. Now they got no choice but to raid. This here's Hancock's war plain and simple."

The camp was quiet. Darkness had closed in around them during the past few minutes. Clark glanced around the circle of young faces, knowing each was considering what they were about to ride into.

"Sergeant Whiting," he said quietly. "Arrange guards for the night."

"Yes, sir." Whiting issued orders, and the troopers moved toward their own tents.

Except for the curvaceous "soldier" beside him.

She was staring into the fire. Decker was staring at her.

"Thanks for the information, Mr. Decker," Clark said, drawing his attention.

"Sure thing. Don't reckon you need guards, though. Most all the raiding's a mite farther west."

"The men will sleep better knowing there are guards on duty," Clark said.

Decker nodded his approval. "I reckon you're right. 'Cept for the ones actually doin' the guardin'." He went back to watching the "soldier."

Clark didn't like the speculative gleam in the old scout's eyes. He was probably thinking she was his mistress, smuggled into camp in uniform.

"Miss Huntington," he said. She turned toward him, sorrow evident in her dark eyes. "Have you met Carl Decker? Mr. Decker, this is Colonel Huntington's daughter."

"Short Deck," Decker croaked, then cleared his throat. "Begging your pardon, ma'am, but is there a reason you're in that getup?"

She gave him her most brilliant smile. Clark could feel the force of it even in profile. "All the ladies are wearing these back east," she said, plucking at the shoulders of the wool blouse. "Though I personally think it needs a little decoration. A couple of bows or something. What do you think?"

Decker grinned, showing tobacco-stained teeth. "Maybe it needs a medal or two."

Her eyes brightened. "Medals! I hadn't thought of that. Do you know where I could get some?"

"If I had any, I'd hand them over right now. Maybe the lieutenant has earned hisself a few."

She turned her smile on Clark. Her eyes were fairly dancing. "What do you think, Lieutenant?"

She was quite a picture, her dark hair curling around her collar and ears, her dimples bracketing smiling pink lips. Every curve of her body outlined by the uniform. "I think you should go back to your wagon."

Her eyes went from teasing to knowing. Damn, she could guess why he wanted her to leave. He didn't like the way Decker watched her. Or the fact that she was practically flirting with the man. She thought he was jealous. He wasn't, of course. She was under his protection, and her flirting made that a more difficult job. He kept his face impassive as she grinned at him.

"Well," she said with a sigh. "I suppose you're right. It was nice meeting you, Short Deck. I'll leave it to Lieutenant Forrester to explain my presence as best he can. Good night."

Out of habit, Clark stood as she stood. Resuming his seat, he tore his eyes away from the retreating figure only to discover that Decker hadn't. "She's traveling with the supply train because the public transportation has temporarily shut down."

Decker didn't turn toward him. "The getup your idea?"

Clark couldn't resist a laugh. "No, that was hers. She believes it won't attract the Indians' attention."

"Sure as hell attracts everybody else's."

"I imagine she's aware of that, as well."

Decker turned and laughed. "She gettin' to ya, Lieutenant?"

Clark had his expression back under control. "She's my commanding officer's daughter."

Decker was still grinning. "You're a better man than I am if you let that stop you."

Clark didn't respond.

"Ah, well," Decker said, coming to his feet with more agility than Clark expected, "I better find my roll and turn in. See ya in the morning, Lieutenant."

"Good night."

Clark gazed into the darkness beyond the fire. He tried to consider what the scout had said, but found himself thinking about Miss Huntington instead. "Medals," he muttered. If he could deliver her to her father without touching her, he would deserve one.

It was best not to even think about her. He would think about Annie; that should bring him back to his senses. Oddly enough, he had a little trouble remembering her face. He remembered the pain when she turned down his proposal, however.

When he got word that his uncle had died, he had requested leave to go home and asked Annie to join him. He had pictured a small wedding with some of his family but had offered to marry her in Dodge before they left. He had known he would be reporting to the new fort upon his return.

She had turned him down. Life as a soldier's wife wasn't for her. She didn't want to move from fort to fort and worry about her husband every time he rode away. And he couldn't blame her.

He didn't feel heartbroken, exactly. But she had been a sweet, quiet, gentle woman who would have made a good helpmate. If she couldn't tolerate his life, what woman could?

He shook off the loneliness. He would miss Annie, of course. And that was why he found his teasing little charge at all attractive. And no doubt that explained why he kept picturing one of his medals dangling from the breast of her uniform blouse.

"He sent out a hunting party," Brooks announced as soon as Rebecca crawled into the seat beside him.

"You're sure?" Rebecca caught sight of the bay as the column started up an incline. He was closer than he had been the day before. Half the troops had been pulled out of formation and positioned along either side of the caravan.

"Sergeant was asking for the best marksmen," Brooks said. "Sent out five. Don't get me wrong, ma'am. I don't begrudge you a good meal. Nor them other ladies neither."

"But?" she prompted.

"But nothing. I'm just talking. What did you think of the old man's story last night? You reckon we're in for trouble?"

Rebecca shrugged. "I don't think we're especially vulnerable. Besides, most of the trouble's west of here."

"Ain't that the way we're going?"

Rebecca had to grin at him. "As a matter of fact, it is. But didn't you join the army to fight Indians?"

"No, ma'am. I joined to eat. And I think I made a mistake."

Rebecca knew the soldier was at least half serious, but she couldn't help laughing. "The army doesn't want you getting too fat for your uniform."

"The army don't have to worry."

He smiled but it wasn't very pleasant. Rebecca turned away, preferring to watch the lieutenant's back. "Oh, look!" she cried. "Another visitor."

As before, Forrester stopped the column and rode forward to meet the stranger. Rebecca wished she was with him to know who it was and what news he might have brought. In a moment the two came riding back, but Forrester didn't signal the column to move. Instead they skirted the troops and cantered toward them.

Rebecca spared the stranger barely a glance. Forrester was such a pleasure to watch. He rode as if he had been born to it, his back straight, his head high. He drew up beside the ambulance with the slightest touch on the reins. She smiled, knowing he had to have seen her watching him.

He showed no sign, however. "Miss Huntington," he said. "Mr. Kolchek has an invitation for you."

Rebecca turned to the stranger. Evidently Forrester hadn't warned him about her attire. It took him a moment to find his voice.

"Miss Huntington," he said, snatching off his hat. "I understand you're one of three women traveling with the soldiers."

"That's right," she said, smiling.

"I own a ranch west a ways. It doubles as a stage station. We'd be pleased to have you ladies as our guests at noon. And the lieutenant, if you can persuade him."

"That's most kind of you," Rebecca said, beaming. "My aunt especially will be grateful for the change of scene, not to mention diet."

"And clothes," Forrester added.

Rebecca sent him a wicked grin.

Kolchek looked from Rebecca to the lieutenant and back. "Yes, well. I best be headed home to see that everything is ready."

He turned his horse and rode away. Forrester turned to follow, but Rebecca stopped him. "Lieutenant. What did he mean if I can persuade you?"

Forrester hesitated. "We'll arrive in a little over an hour. You ladies might want to change as we travel. I'll try to give you plenty of time to enjoy Mr.

Kolchek's hospitality, but you can't have the whole of the afternoon.''

He started away again.

''Wait!'' He was polite enough to turn back, and his irritation was barely visible. ''Aren't you eating with us?''

''That depends.'' This time he turned away with enough resolve she didn't try to call him back.

She sank down into the seat and watched him go. In a moment they were moving again.

''He'll eat with you,'' Brooks said, startling her. She had nearly forgotten him.

''Depends on what?'' she wondered aloud. Didn't he want to eat with her?

Brooks shrugged. ''Care to make a friendly bet?'' he asked in a low voice.

She laughed. ''Want me to bring you a steak if you're right?''

''I got more on my mind than food. I was thinking more like a kiss.''

Rebecca's stomach turned queasy. She tried to laugh it off. ''What do I get if I win?''

He was quiet for a moment than offered softly, ''You could bet the same thing.''

''No deal,'' she said, trying not to sound as revolted as she felt. ''Gambling's frowned on in the army.''

''Is kissing, too?'' he whispered. ''We could skip the bet and go straight to the payoff.''

"I need to go change." She rose to climb over the seat, taking more care than usual not to touch him.

"I'll be thinking of you," he whispered.

Rebecca scrambled under the canvas and tied the front flap in place. She turned to find Belle and Alicia staring at her. Had they been listening to her conversation with Brooks? They could hardly blame *her* for what he said.

"Did you hear we've been invited to dine at a stage station?" she asked, making her way to the back of the rocking wagon. It seemed unbearably close. She pulled aside the canvas to let in a hint of a breeze, realizing how peculiar that might seem after tying the front flap.

"It's not proper," Aunt Belle said.

"Proper? Aunt Belle, I'm sure they invite most travelers to eat with them."

"I mean the way you talk to that lieutenant. You are far too familiar. He's bound to remember how you made eyes at him on the train."

Rebecca resisted a sigh of relief. If she had heard Brooks she wouldn't be so concerned about her behavior toward Forrester. From experience she knew the best tactic with Aunt Belle. "I'm sorry," she said, letting her head hang slightly. "I forgot myself. I'll try to act with more decorum in the future."

"Good," stated Belle, evidently willing to accept her vow at face value. "Now, I'm ready to get out of these awful clothes. We've only an hour to make ourselves presentable.''

Approximately an hour later the ambulance rolled to a stop in front of Kolchek's station. Rebecca got her first glimpse of the long low building when Brooks came behind to help them out of the wagon. Aunt Belle had forbidden either her or Alicia to part the canvas for so much as a peek for fear their dresses would get dusty. ''It's hard enough dressing in such a confining space without dust billowing in as well,'' she had said.

The house was built of rough-hewn wood and completely devoid of paint. The roof didn't even seem to be level. Alicia stepped up beside Rebecca as she studied the building. ''That's ghastly,'' she whispered.

''Rustic,'' Rebecca corrected.

Aunt Belle made an audible gasp as she climbed from the wagon. ''My,'' she said, joining the girls. The wagon clattered out of the yard, and Belle looked after it with something akin to panic.

A large woman emerged from one of the three doors that ran along the front of the house. Shading her eyes with one hand she waved with the other. ''Come on in out of the sun and have a cool drink. Dinner'll be ready in no time.''

''It's bound to be cooler inside,'' Belle said, stepping forward. Rebecca and Alicia followed her onto the porch.

After they had all introduced themselves, Mrs. Kolchek expressed a need to get back to the kitchen. "You folks just make yourselves at home."

"I'd like to walk around a little," Rebecca said. "I'll only be a few minutes."

Alicia touched her mother's arm. "I'll go with Rebecca and see that she doesn't take too long."

"Good idea." Belle followed the woman into the station.

"I hope you don't mind," Alicia said. "I wanted to apologize for letting Mother overhear your conversation with your lieutenant. I parted the canvas to see why we had stopped. It muffles sound quite effectively the rest of the time."

"Don't give it another thought," Rebecca said, turning in a slow circle. Where was the lieutenant, and what could she have done to assure his presence? She made out the soldier's camp nearer the creek.

"What is there to look at?" Alicia asked. "Or should I say look for?"

"Horses," Rebecca said, pointing. "I want to look at the horses."

"Certainly," Alicia muttered, following along. "And your lieutenant will see you standing out here and won't be able to resist coming in."

Rebecca grinned. "Do you think he'll notice me?"

"If Mother had known how bright that red dress

was, she would have objected. It looked more subdued in the wagon.''

At the corral fence Rebecca climbed onto the low-
est rung and reached her hand toward an iron-gray
gelding. ''Come here, boy,'' she coaxed.

''Rebecca.'' There was a note of warning in Alicia's voice.

''He won't hurt me,'' she murmured in the same
soft tone. ''Will you, handsome? Come on. I just
want to talk to you.''

Rebecca's father had taught her about horses, and
the gelding was a beautiful animal. He tossed his
head and stepped closer.

''Come on, sweetheart.''

The horse took the last few steps and let Rebecca
rub its nose and neck.

''I see your charm works with horses, too.''

At the softly accented words Rebecca spun around,
nearly falling off the fence. Strong hands caught her
and settled her on the ground. He backed away much
too quickly.

''I didn't mean to startle you.'' The light in his
eyes made a lie of the statement.

''Why of course you didn't, Lieutenant,'' she said,
giving him her biggest smile. ''I'm lucky you moved
quickly enough to catch me.''

''My pleasure, ma'am.''

Alicia had to clear her throat twice before either
of them turned toward her.

Chapter Four

Clark tore his eyes away from the smiling beauty.

"Perhaps we should go in," the younger girl said.

"Of course. Ladies." He offered each an arm.

"Tell me, Lieutenant," Miss Huntington began, acting as if she were strolling down a city sidewalk. "What exactly was your presence here for dinner dependent on?"

"The hunting party," he said. At her questioning look, he added, "They brought down a good-sized deer. The men are dressing it out now. There'll be enough for tonight as well as their noon meal."

"And if the hunters hadn't gotten back in time, or had come in empty-handed?"

"I'd be enjoying the government's famous pork with the rest of the men."

"You're an honorable man, Lieutenant," Miss Huntington said, turning toward him as she stepped onto the sloping porch. Her smile seemed more sincere than flirtatious, but with this young lady, he didn't trust his perceptions.

"I hope so, ma'am. But it isn't so much honor as common sense."

He let the ladies precede him into the squat little station. The room was smoky from oil lamps and cigars. Mrs. Evans, sitting in a high-backed chair, seemed relieved to see them.

"Our host has gone to help bring in the meal," she said. "It seems some of our food was cooked 'out back' as he put it. I've been afraid to look out and see what he meant."

The younger ladies indicated a desire to wash, and their senior offered to show them where she had earlier been directed. Alone, Clark looked around the crudely furnished room. There wasn't much to recommend the place, except Kolchek himself. Clark had met him twice before, and Sergeant Whiting knew him well. He had the reputation of knowing everything that went on in his portion of the state.

In a moment the ladies returned. Clark found it difficult to make polite conversation when his eyes kept returning to the beauty in the red dress. Her short curls were even more incongruous with the elegant attire than they were with the men's trousers. He refused, however, to feel guilty.

The Kolcheks joined them, and in a few minutes they were seated before a veritable feast. Kolchek pointed out buffalo roast, venison steaks and his own cured ham, as well as early peas and last year's sweet potatoes.

Once the women were deep in conversation, Clark asked Kolchek for any news of the uprising.

"Some raids," he said softly, obviously not wanting to concern the ladies. "Railroad workers west of Ellsworth, mostly. They seem to know that track means the end of their hunting ground."

"They can't expect to stop the construction of the railroad," Clark said.

"They have, at least for now. They don't look at progress quite the way we do. Besides, they've been promised things they never got, and they're mighty sore."

Clark's eyes went across the table, as they did every few seconds. This time they locked with Miss Huntington's. The other ladies were discussing recipes, but her attention had shifted.

She turned from him to their host. "Why won't the government give them what they want?"

"They want Kansas, ma'am. And Nebraska, Colorado, the whole of the western plains. It may be theirs by rights, but they've already lost it."

Clark wondered what she was thinking as she returned her attention to her plate. Next he wondered why he cared. Her only interest would be for her own comfort.

His suspicion was confirmed a moment later. She raised her head, her sparkling smile back in place. "I noticed some beautiful horses in your corral, Mr. Kolchek. Do they belong to you or the stage line?"

"Some of both out there, though the best ones are mine."

Clark stood, excused himself and promised to send the wagon in half an hour. Getting the ladies' assurances that they would be ready, he thanked the Kolcheks and left.

Out in the sunlight again, he wondered why he gave Miss Huntington more than passing notice. Why was he curious about her opinions? She probably didn't have any beyond what she had been told. Why was he fascinated by the slightest change in her expressive lips?

He swung into the saddle and turned to gaze for a moment at the station. He had tasted those lips once and wanted to again. His attraction was purely physical. He only pretended there was something more to excuse his reaction.

Even that realization filled him with some alarm. Since when had physical attraction left him searching for excuses? And this woman had already threatened his career. He should keep an eye on her the same way he was watching a distant storm cloud. And for precisely the same reasons.

The door opened, and Miss Huntington stepped out. Kolchek was right behind her. Clark turned his horse away, but the flash of red against the gray, drab building stayed in his mind.

* * *

Rebecca brushed her hand over the neck of her newly acquired horse. While the others sat on the porch and chatted, she led the gelding around the dusty yard, stroked him, talked to him, everything but rode him. Not in this dress. At least not with this saddle.

Finally, Brooks drove the ambulance into the yard. While he helped Belle and Alicia into the wagon, Rebecca tied her horse on behind.

As soon as she was inside, Rebecca enlisted Alicia's help in getting out of the dress. She was slipping into the pants when the wagon stopped. "Find out what's going on," she said.

Alicia pulled the canvas aside a fraction. "Why are we stopped?" she asked. She turned back to Rebecca. "We're waiting for the rest to start moving."

"How much time does it look like I'll have?" Rebecca asked, hastily buttoning the uniform blouse.

"I don't know." With a resigned sigh, Alicia returned to the crack in the canvas. "Just a few minutes."

"Minutes is fine," Rebecca said, pulling on her socks. "I was afraid I only had seconds."

"I think this is positively disgraceful," Aunt Belle said. "I for one, intend to continue wearing my dress until evening. I can't believe you're not eager to do the same."

Rebecca tossed her a quick smile as she hastily

tied the boy's work shoes she had bought at Fort Riley and grabbed her hat. "If you have any problems, let Brooks know. If he has to pull out of line, have him send one of the soldiers to find me."

"You'll be in front flirting shamelessly with that officer. Honestly, Rebecca—"

But Rebecca scrambled out the back of the ambulance before her aunt could finish. "I don't know what's to become of you," she mimicked under her breath. She untied the gelding and led him away from the wagon, wanting to take a little time to get reacquainted before she tried to mount him.

The ambulance rolled forward just as she sprang into the saddle. The gelding tossed his head and circled once before giving in to her lead. She put him at a canter and soon joined the lieutenant at the front of the column.

"Afternoon, Miss Huntington," he said, barely giving her a glance.

She smiled at him, not revealing her disappointment. She had hoped to surprise him. Of course, he had such a poker face she might not have known it if she had. How could he be so aloof?

"Afternoon, Miss Huntington," called the sergeant riding on the other side of Forrester. "You picked a fine horse there."

"Why, thank you, Mr. Whiting. I think he'll do nicely."

"Kolchek's known around here for his horses.

He's careful what he buys and likes to do his own training.''

"He said this one's a four-year-old he bought as a colt.''

Rebecca watched Forrester's profile as she talked to the sergeant. She truly loved that jaw. And the straight line of his nose and nearly straight brow were appealing as well. His gray eyes flicked in her direction, and she wondered if he sensed her scrutiny.

"How did you pay for the horse?'' he asked, his eyes on the trail ahead.

Was the question simply a way to join the conversation, or was something else implied? She kept her voice light as she answered, "My mother left me some money. I closed out the account before we left Chicago, and I took some of it with me to dinner intending to buy a horse if one was available. So it wasn't quite the impulsive decision it may have appeared. Did you think I charmed the horse away from him, Lieutenant?''

His head actually turned in her direction then. His eyes shot her a warning, and her grin broadened. *You don't want me to tease you in front of the troops? Then let me get you alone.*

"I know Kolchek pretty well, ma'am,'' Sergeant Whiting said. "He loves his horses, and he knows the value of a dollar. I can't imagine him giving a horse away. Though if anyone could charm him, you could, Miss Huntington.''

"Why, thank you, Sergeant," Rebecca said, still grinning at the lieutenant.

He turned away, leaving her to study his profile again. The only hint of his annoyance was in the compression of his lips. She didn't really want to make him angry with her, but it was hard to resist teasing someone so stiff, someone so determined to ignore her. She could guess that he regretted even speaking to her. He didn't again for quite some time.

She and the sergeant spoke occasionally about the names of the creeks they crossed, and other landmarks in the monotonous plain.

Rebecca was in heaven. She loved riding, she loved the prairie and had longed for it the past six years. And she liked being near good-looking men even if they pretended to ignore her.

The last thought made her smile. "Isn't it a perfect day?"

"Unless you take that storm into account." The lieutenant pointed ahead and to the left.

Rebecca looked at the deep blue settling on the south-western horizon and knew it meant rain, possibly wind and hail as well. She sighed dramatically. "There's only one cloud in the sky, Lieutenant. Does that define the whole day?"

"My guess, ma'am, is that it will pretty well define this evening."

Rebecca laughed. She couldn't help it. Forrester worked so hard at being serious. "Right now, the sun is shining. And whether it rains tonight or not, I'll be closer to home than I was yesterday."

"That brings up a question I've been meaning to ask you, Miss Huntington." He didn't turn toward her for more than a glance from the corner of his eye. "You said you had been gone for six years. How—"

Rebecca interrupted. "When did I say that, Lieutenant?" *On the train.* Of course he remembered, too.

He opened his mouth, closed it, swallowed once. "Early in our association."

Rebecca grinned. He clearly wanted to forget the incident. She wanted to make it just as clear that she liked remembering it. "Yes," she murmured. "I did say six years."

It was a moment before he returned to his question. "How is it that you're *returning* home when Fort Hays didn't exist six years ago, or even six months ago?"

Ah, was he wondering if she had been lying to him? "That's easy, Lieutenant." She swept her arm across the horizon then held her hand to her heart. "The prairie is my home."

"Very poetic, but it doesn't answer my question." There was the barest sparkle of humor in his eyes when he glanced toward her.

"I've lived in forts all over the West. Wherever my father is, is home. I don't know why I didn't explain that at the time, unless I was distracted."

He missed her wide-eyed, innocent expression entirely by refusing to look at her. She rode in cheerful silence until they made camp at what Whiting called Spring Creek.

After Rebecca had fed and watered the gray gelding and picketed him with the cavalry horses, she made her way to the ambulance. Evening was coming on quickly, and there was a definite smell of rain in the air. The campsite was set up but empty. "Aunt Belle," she called. "Alicia?"

"They went down to the creek to wash."

She spun around to find Victor Brooks standing directly behind her.

"I was hoping you would turn up before they got back," he said. "I missed you this afternoon."

"That's sweet of you," she said. She walked around the camp pretending to study its layout as a way of moving away from him. It didn't work; he soon intercepted her.

"I can be sweeter still," he murmured.

"Mr. Brooks," she said, choosing now to stand her ground. "I'm afraid you've made a mistake."

"Is that so?" He stopped too close to her. He was taller than she had noticed, broader. The tension in his posture, the sharpness of the softly spoken words, even his smell seemed threatening. Alcohol, she realized.

"Yes, it's so," she said firmly. "I've given you no reason to expect..."

He touched her cheek lightly. She drew back and watched his brows come together in a scowl. "You gave me every reason to expect plenty. All your bright smiles." His voice lowered as he added, "Your whispers."

He leaned in for a kiss, and she stepped away. "No," she said again, crossing her arms in front of her. "I intended to be friendly. That's all."

"You know that's not all you intended. We ain't got time for you to play coy. The others'll be back any minute." He grabbed her shoulders, pulling her roughly toward him.

Rebecca jerked her hands upward, intending to push him away. One curled fist caught him on the chin. He swore and shoved her away. She staggered but caught her balance, eyeing him warily as he tested his tongue for blood.

"You tease!" he croaked. "Ain't I good enough no more? Since you got a horse now, you got your eye on a officer like Dixie Boy? Well, don't worry, *lady,* I understand completely."

He turned on his heel and stalked toward his messmates' fire. Rebecca let out a deep breath. Had he really interpreted her friendly smiles as flirting? Perhaps he had seen what he wanted to see. She sank into one of the folding chairs. Could flirting have become second nature to her until she did it without realizing it?

A few minutes later her aunt and cousin returned.

They were both in the dresses they had worn at noon. "Don't say anything," Aunt Belle said, marching past her. "I will not believe that there are Indians lurking about in this weather." She climbed into the ambulance and let the canvas drop back into place.

Alicia came to sit beside Rebecca. "I thought it would be all right," she said. "I didn't tell her what you said about the lieutenant's bluff."

"I suppose it would be cruel to insist that she wear the pants," Rebecca conceded, trying not to smile. "When I hit on the idea, I didn't realize she would look on them as torture."

"Yes, you did," Alicia said.

Rebecca tried to look hurt. "I know," she said, brightening. "I'll ask the lieutenant if he thinks there are Indians watching us yet. If he says no, we can tell your mother it's safe to wear dresses for a day or so. Perhaps she would roll up the canvas or even ride with the driver part of the day. That would give you some relief as well."

"And what will be your excuse to continue in the pants?"

"I'll be riding horseback. Oh, here comes dinner. I'll get your mother." She rose quickly and went to the wagon, not wanting to be left alone at the table if Alicia ran the errand. She coaxed her aunt out and walked back to the table with her, grateful that Brooks left a moment after she arrived.

* * *

Clark finished the dinner his striker had brought and moved the dishes to the corner of his field desk. As he opened the box that held his journal, he heard the first smattering of raindrops on the roof of the tent. The flap was propped up with poles forming an awning over the open doorway and letting in the fresh scent of rain.

Under the journal was the leather-bound case his cousin had given him. His fingers caressed it for a second, then he set the journal aside and lifted the case from the box. At his desk, he opened it.

The hand-carved chess set had belonged to his uncle. He hadn't seen it for years. "You were the only one who ever beat him," his cousin had said. "He wanted you to have it."

So he had taken the set and thanked his cousin. With the funeral, the train, and now the Indian uprising, he had nearly forgotten he had it.

The striker appeared at his door, shaking rain from his hat.

"Come in, Powers." Clark nodded toward the dishes. "These could have waited until morning."

"I wanted to see if you needed anything else, sir. Besides, I've been hot and dry so long I hardly mind the rain."

At that moment, the sprinkle turned into a downpour, sending torrents of rain against the roof and back wall of the tent. "That's good," Clark said, "because it sounds like you're going to get wet."

"May I come in?" a female voice called above the roar.

Clark turned toward the doorway. Miss Huntington had obviously been caught in the deluge. She was soaked from head to foot, her hat drooping with the weight of the rain. Her face, when she removed the hat, bore its usual sunny smile.

Clark stood. "Mr. Powers, fetch a blanket from my cot," he said with a glance at the man. "You should be in your wagon, Miss Huntington."

"It's a little late now." She shook out the hat and set it on the ground just inside the tent. As Powers brought the blanket she shook her head, sending tiny drops of water flying off the tips of her curls. "I'll get your blanket wet."

"I have another," he said. "Did you need something, Miss Huntington?"

She let Powers wrap the blanket around her shoulders, offering him a soft, "Thank you," and a smile. "As a matter of fact, I have a question." She moved toward him. "Do you play chess?"

"You risked drowning to ask me that?"

She laughed. "Of course not. What a lovely set." She lifted a knight from the case on his desk. "My question has to do with Aunt Belle and Indians. Do you play?"

"Yes. Aunt Belle and Indians?" Clark was aware of Powers' curiosity. He was also aware of the danger of being alone with this woman. News of that would travel as quickly and do more damage than any gossip Powers might spread about their conversation.

"Aunt Belle wants to know if you think there are Indians watching us." She put the knight back and picked up a bishop. "Aren't these hand carved?"

"Yes. No." He shook his head. This woman could confuse him like no other. "No Indians are watching us, and yes, they're hand carved."

"Shall we play a game while I wait for the rain to let up?"

Clark opened his mouth to mention that the rain might not let up before morning. He was afraid that wouldn't deter her. "All right."

Powers stepped forward with another folding chair for Miss Huntington, and in a moment she was seated across the desk from Clark. Powers reached for the dishes. "If there's nothing else…"

"Have you had your own dinner, Mr. Powers?" Clark asked.

"Yes, sir."

"Then have a seat."

"Sir?"

"Until the rain lets up, then you can see Miss Huntington back to her wagon."

"Yes, sir." The striker was clearly bewildered, but he did as he was instructed.

Miss Huntington knew exactly what he was doing. She gave him a mischievous grin as she pulled the four pieces of the game board from under the chessmen and fitted them together.

"So," she asked, "who carved these pieces?"

"My uncle." Clark sank into the chair. The devil's own temptation was sitting across from him, mixing her own image and scent with his older memories of his uncle's chess set. He should have refused. As he watched her put the pieces on their proper squares he wondered how he thought he could have.

He reminded himself that she wasn't the perfection she appeared. She was spoiled and manipulative. She would watch his honor, his career, his life go up in smoke if it suited her purposes. Just as he thought he had that clear in his mind, she looked up and smiled her captivating smile.

"Shall we flip to see who plays first?" she asked.

"Be my guest, Miss Huntington."

"Call me Rebecca," she said, moving her knight. He shook his head, but she persisted. "We want to keep this a friendly game, don't we, Clark?"

He had already had a taste of her friendly games. The stakes were too high, and the odds were in her favor. He should stick to chess. He moved a pawn and found himself saying, "As you wish, Rebecca."

She made her move, then taking the ends of the blanket that was still around her shoulders, she rubbed briefly at her hair. She tossed her head and ran her fingers through the short locks, loosening the curls.

"I can't believe I cut your hair." The comment seemed to go from his heart to his lips, bypassing his brain.

She laughed, tossing her head again. "I like it."

"I don't think that's what your father will say." Thinking of the colonel should help him keep his wits about him. He tried to look at the board, but his eyes were drawn back to the dark curls.

She simply shrugged. "He won't even notice."

He raised his brows in surprise, causing her to grin. "It's your move," she said.

He played. "How could he not notice?"

She bit her lip as she studied the board. It was a habit he had never noticed before. Why should it be at all charming?

With a smile, she moved a piece, then answered, "My hair was shorter than this when I was growing up. Mother was terrified that I would be scalped. Her theory was that cutting my hair decreased its value as a trophy. She trimmed it nearly every week until I was twelve."

He thought of how his female cousins and their friends would have rejected a girl with shorn locks. Perhaps her flirting stemmed from a desire to prove her beauty. He turned his attention to the board, more from a need to look away from her than from any interest in the game. After he played, he asked, "What happened when you were twelve?"

"My mother died." He would have liked to have

seen her eyes, but she was bent over the board. "Two years later the war started. So many of the troops were pulled out of the western forts Father didn't think it was safe for me. I went to live with his sister's family in Chicago. My uncle died last winter, and now Aunt Belle and Alicia are coming home with me."

She moved a piece. When she looked up her smile was in place. "There you have my life story."

He gazed at her a moment. A trace of sorrow was visible behind the smile. "I'm surprised you're so eager to return to life at a frontier fort."

"Best possible way to grow up."

He was startled by her conviction. "Poor housing. Virtually no education available. Not to mention the fact that there are dangers in the area or the fort would not be there."

She shrugged. "Children don't care about those things. It's your move."

He stared at her a moment before turning his attention to the board.

"Children," she said, "love freedom, and sunshine, and riding, and…having donkeys for pets, and parades every day. And happy parents. That was my childhood."

"Life will be different now that you're grown."

"I know," she said, the grin returning. "I've found other enjoyable activities."

The sparkle in her eyes left little doubt of what

those activities included. He felt a need to distract her. He hadn't forgotten about Powers, even if she had—or more likely didn't care. "You'll be running your father's household, managing at least one servant, and directing the social life of the fort."

She wrinkled her nose, and he held back a smile. "Aunt Belle will be in charge of all that, even if I wanted the job. Especially if I wanted the job."

Clark gave in and smiled. "What will you do?"

She shrugged, leaning forward to move a piece. "I can teach, improve the deplorable education you mentioned."

Clark couldn't resist a soft chuckle.

"What?" She sounded offended, but a smile still graced her lips. "You don't think I could teach?"

"I'm having trouble picturing it, ma'am."

"Shows what you know. It's your move."

He studied the board but knowing those sparkling eyes and sweet lips were right in front of him made it difficult. He found himself playing as quickly as possible so he could return his attention to her face. Such a mischievous smile had never shone from the face of any schoolteacher he had seen. "So how will you convince anyone to hire you?"

She blinked her eyes with feigned innocence. "You mean, convince Daddy?"

He nodded. "I see your point."

She tipped her head and a speculative light came

into her eyes. "Your problem, Clark, is that you don't have enough respect for me."

Shocked, Clark started to protest, but she raised her hand.

"I don't mean the courteous respect that a gentleman shows a lady. No one could fault you there. I'm talking about respect for me as a person, respect for my intelligence, for my opinion. I could be a very logical person, Lieutenant, if it mattered. But it never does."

Clark stared at her. He had a sinking feeling she was right. If he denied it, wouldn't he be claiming he respected her to win her favor, the same kind of manipulation he believed her guilty of? An apology seemed in order, but he had no idea where to start.

To his amazement and relief, a smile returned to her lips. "Of course, I'm basing this on my observation of men in general, including my father. I could be wrong about you."

Clark opened his mouth to speak and closed it again. Was she offering him a lifeline or a noose? He was afraid to respond.

She seemed pleased to have struck him speechless. "I believe it's my turn," she said, bending over the board. "Let me see...oh, yes." She moved a piece. He didn't know which one; his eyes were on her as they had been since she invaded his tent.

She sat back, satisfied. "Check."

He looked down at the board, scarcely comprehending.

"Mate."

His eyes flew back to her face. She wasn't gloating, at least not as much as he expected. He nodded. "I concede." He hoped she understood he meant more than the chess game.

"I believe the rain has nearly stopped."

He hadn't noticed when the pounding on the canvas had lessened. He came to his feet when she did. "Take the blanket with you in case it's only a momentary reprieve."

"Thank you, Clark. A rematch tomorrow?"

He should refuse. Her presence was too upsetting. In the face of her questioning smile, he found himself relenting. "I'm afraid my ego demands it, ma'am."

"Rebecca," she corrected softly.

Powers had stepped through the opening and was waiting under the awning, holding her hat. She followed him, readjusting the blanket around her shoulders, smiling sweetly when she took the hat. In a moment she had disappeared into the darkness.

"Rebecca," he whispered. The girl was full of surprises, but his own behavior was no less baffling. He had barely made it through her visit with his control intact before he consented to a rematch. Was he testing his own willpower? Or had she already destroyed it?

He should be furious with her. She had used blackmail to win a place on his supply caravan. She used flirtation to win a game of chess. What would she win tomorrow?

And why wasn't that apprehension he felt curling through his bloodstream?

Chapter Five

Rebecca couldn't sleep. She stared at the darkness above her and tried not to disturb the others in the wagon. Why had she said those things to Clark? What had she hoped to accomplish by turning serious? Men didn't like that!

She had intended to flirt with him just a little, then go. But the rain had surprised her, and the chess set had drawn her. And how she loved the way his brows shot up when he was surprised! Clearly that had been her downfall. He refused to show any response to her smiles or quips, refused, in short, to be dazzled. But he couldn't hide surprise.

Still, she shouldn't have said he didn't respect her. And she shouldn't have beat him at chess. She had momentarily lost sight of her goal. Which was, she reminded herself firmly, simply to enjoy his attention for a time. She knew how to get and keep a man's attention, or had always thought she did. And turning serious was *not* the way. He was probably a lost cause now.

The disappointment she felt was inappropriate. He meant no more to her than any of the others. If it was over, she would forget him. Being near him the next few days wouldn't matter. It never had before. In fact, it was probably better that it was over sooner rather than later. Once before she had made the mistake of continuing a flirtation too long, and the young man had begun to imagine she wanted something permanent.

She rolled to her side and tried to picture Clark asking to marry her. She couldn't. In fact, it was probably the farthest thing from his mind. Another possibility struck her like a blow. Perhaps he didn't pretend to ignore her; perhaps she didn't interest him at all.

The pain she felt was merely her stung pride, of course. *He* didn't matter any more than any of the others. And she would prove it to herself in the morning. She would return his blanket before they left camp and while she was at it, tell him she had changed her mind about the chess game. She would tell him she had something to do, something that would sound boring—like mending. Then he would know how unimportant he was to her. And she would know it, too.

With that resolution in mind, she closed her eyes

but it took some time before her mind gave in to sleep.

The camp was filled with activity when Rebecca made her way to Clark's tent. She blamed her melancholy mood on all the sleep she had missed while she sorted out her feelings for Clark—or rather her lack of them.

This wouldn't be difficult, she told herself. She would simply smile and be apologetic. She couldn't join him for chess this evening. Maybe another time.

She had already pasted on the smile when she came to a sudden stop. Her hands clenched around the folded blanket she held close to her breast. Clark stood outside his tent, more than half turned away from her. His suspenders dangled at his sides and a towel was slung over an otherwise bare shoulder. He had fastened a small mirror to a tent post and was shaving that gorgeous jaw.

Her mouth dropped open and her throat went dry. Her fingers itched to touch his cheek. With each scrape of the razor she felt her knees tremble. He raised his chin to shave his neck, bringing his jawbone into greater prominence. She swallowed a groan.

He shaved above his lip, his chin. She touched her own chin and licked her dry lips. When he went to work on the cheek away from her she considered circling his camp to improve her view.

She couldn't, of course. He might catch her reflection in the mirror. So she watched the play of muscles across his back instead. She tried to swallow and discovered she couldn't.

When he set the razor aside, she turned and fled. As she neared the ambulance, she slowed to a nervous walk. She hadn't spoken to him because she hadn't wanted to startle him; he might have cut himself. It wasn't true that she couldn't have spoken if she had tried. Besides, she hadn't wanted to embarrass him. Why, they both would have been mortified if he had seen her while he was without his shirt.

At the wagon, she sank into a camp chair. Her stomach was trembling—from the run, of course. She had barely pulled herself together when she heard Aunt Belle's voice and Alicia's murmured reply. She had forgotten about them entirely.

The two ladies appeared around a nearby tent, followed by Brooks bearing their breakfast. "Mr. Brooks and his friends have been showing us how they cook breakfast over a campfire," Alicia said.

Aunt Belle huffed. "I bought a few eggs from Mrs. Kolchek, and I wanted to see they were cooked properly."

Rebecca nodded at both explanations. She remained seated, careful not to make eye contact with Brooks. It wasn't until she tried to move her chair closer to the table that she realized she still held the blanket. There was nothing to do but rise and put it in the wagon.

"I thought you were returning that," Aunt Belle said, taking her seat and dismissing Brooks with a careless wave. At the same time Alicia gave the soldier an apologetic smile.

Rebecca thanked him without quite looking at him. "He was busy," she answered her aunt. "I would have left it anyway, but I didn't want to interrupt."

Delicious images flooded her mind accompanied by a sense of anticipation. How foolish! She wasn't going to go spy on him again, tempting as the thought was. She was going to put him out of her mind.

"Get that driver fellow to return it for you."

She looked up, startled by her aunt's suggestion. The blanket being returned by a soldier instead of personally would convey the message quite effectively. Especially since she didn't trust herself.

"Good idea, Aunt Belle," Rebecca said, reaching for her coffee cup. "I'll do that when he returns for the skillet."

She caught a glimpse of Alicia's disbelieving look, and tossed her a bright smile. When they had a moment alone, she would have to explain to the girl about ending a flirtation.

"I was kinda hoping the colonel's daughter would come ride with us again," Sergeant Whiting commented.

Clark wasn't sure if he agreed or not. It was mid-morning, and he had been practically bracing himself for her appearance since their departure. The sense of disappointment he felt was merely concern, surely. At least when she was with him, he knew she wasn't causing trouble somewhere else. "Perhaps we bored her yesterday."

"Speak for yourself, sir."

Clark cast Whiting a sidelong glance. "I take it I'm boring you this morning, Sergeant."

"Off the record, sir?"

Clark grinned and nodded.

"You're not as pretty as she is."

"I imagined it was something like that."

"But seriously, sir, do you suppose that gelding of hers coulda thrown her? He's a spirited horse, and she's a city girl."

Clark didn't think it was likely. He knew she was an experienced rider. Odd that he would treasure a bit of personal information about her that Whiting didn't share. He shook off the thought.

Unless Rebecca had dropped behind the caravan, there would have been someone nearby to help her in the chance she had taken a fall. If she had been injured he would have been alerted. Still, he couldn't help wondering what she was up to.

"Sergeant, why don't you ride back and find out?"

"Yes, sir!" The sergeant wheeled his mount away

from the column, kicking up globs of mud, and galloped toward the wagons.

Clark chuckled softly. Even the old sergeant wasn't immune to the lady's charms. But there was more to her than dimpled smiles and flashing eyes. He found himself looking forward to another conversation over his uncle's chessboard.

There wouldn't be a repeat of last night's game. He vowed not to be surprised by anything she said. And he would also keep at least part of his mind on the game. He thought of several possible topics of conversation and found himself hoping the sergeant would invite her forward.

After several long minutes, Clark began to wonder if he should have been more specific in his order to the sergeant. He hadn't stipulated that the man return. He was considering stopping the column and reminding the sergeant that he was still on duty, when the man in question reined in beside him. Alone.

There he rode in silence.

Clark felt his teeth grind together and made a conscious effort to relax his jaw. She was merely a traveler in his protection. The sergeant had checked on her well-being. He evidently had nothing to report. But where was she? What was she doing? With whom was she riding? He'd be damned before he'd ask.

He heard the sergeant chuckle and turned to him,

keeping his face carefully blank. "She's fine, sir," Whiting said.

"I assumed as much." He turned away.

"Any questions, sir?" He sounded as if he was struggling to keep from laughing.

"You said she was fine. I'm no longer worried about her."

Whiting laughed then. "That's good, sir. I just thought you might want to know that she's riding back yonder alongside the ambulance. The sides are rolled up for once, and she's talking to her aunt and that pretty little cousin of hers. Their driver makes a remark now and then. Oh, and Miss Huntington casts a lotta longing glances toward the front of the line, though she pretends not to."

"Thank you, Mr. Whiting," Clark interjected.

"What I can't figure is, if she wishes she was riding up here, why's she back there?"

"Thank you, Mr. Whiting," Clark repeated, more forcefully.

"Just thought you'd like to know, being concerned about her and all."

Clark clenched his jaw, hoping Whiting would take his silence as a hint to be quiet as well. His hopes were dashed in a second.

"Did you hurt her feelings last night, sir?"

"Mr. Whiting," Clark said, putting the force of his rank behind his words. "That is none of your business."

Whiting was undaunted. "I only ask because I know she was friendly yesterday, spent a little time in your tent last night." At Clark's glare he hastened to add, "Properly chaperoned, of course, sir."

"Sergeant—"

"I only mention it, sir, because even if you don't think you said anything wrong, hell, even if she insulted you, you're the one who's gonna have to apologize. I wanted to be sure you understood that, sir."

"Well, I thank you for the advice, Mr. Whiting, but let me offer some of my own. Don't get involved in my love life. You'll be bored to death."

Whiting chuckled. "You might be right, sir. You see, I know about that little waitress, Annie."

Clark stifled a groan. Of course, he should have been prepared. Soldiers were worse gossips than a bunch of old ladies.

"You knew she got married shortly after you went East?"

Clark shook his head briefly. He hadn't known, though he supposed he shouldn't have been surprised. She hadn't indicated an aversion to marriage, only marriage to a soldier. He felt again a pang of disappointment knowing he would never see her again, but it was more from the loss of something familiar than any deep sorrow.

Whiting brought him out of his reverie. "Now that was one boring love affair, sir. I'd have—"

"Sergeant Whiting."

"Yes, sir?"

"Shut up. And that's an order."

"Yes, sir."

Clark could see Whiting's grin out of the corner of his eye. He didn't care. As long as the conversation ended before Whiting found a way to bring it back to speculation about Rebecca Huntington.

The lieutenant sent me back to ask after you and the ladies. The lieutenant... The lieutenant...

Rebecca tried to shake off the sergeant's statement that kept repeating itself in her mind. She shouldn't be delighted that the lieutenant was thinking of her. She was supposed to be forgetting about him. It was just that she kept forgetting that.

Riding near Aunt Belle didn't help anything either. The woman was skilled in every style of complaining; normal conversation was lost on her. Alicia might have been fun, but what could they talk about within earshot of Aunt Belle and Brooks? Trees?

Incredibly enough that was exactly what they had been discussing. She left Alicia and Brooks to carry on without her as she watched the front of the column longingly. Why was she riding back here when she could be alongside the lieutenant? Clark, she reminded herself with a smile. He had been so carefully serious last night, but he had consented to the use of their first names—reluctantly.

It would be nice to have some personal information to go with that first name. She had told him some of her childhood, but he had said next to nothing about himself. She began speculating on what approach would be most likely to gain her the information she sought, when she remembered it was over. She wouldn't be coaxing anything out of him ever again.

She shifted in the saddle, feeling a desire to kick the gelding into a run. She had been unusually restless all day. Maybe it was the mud. She was tired of slogging through it. She was tired of watching it coat the wagon's wheels. She was tired of hearing her aunt complain about how it had ruined her shoes this morning.

Ah, but the rain itself had been a wonderful thing. It had kept her in Clark's tent. She shook herself. She had decided last night that that had been a mistake. She had ruined any chance of dazzling him again, and she was now determined to forget him.

But even if she couldn't dazzle him, she could ride with him. Her horse was supposed to set her free, and here she was, as trapped as ever. She glanced at her companions. They were silent now, all staring straight ahead. She should excuse herself and ride up beside the sergeant. She might even succeed in making Clark jealous.

Darn! She had forgotten again! She didn't want to make him jealous. It was as if part of her brain wasn't listening to the rest and kept offering foolish suggestions. And it wasn't because she needed an alternative to the lieutenant; she had often gone weeks without a beau.

With a sigh, she acknowledged the truth. Clark Forrester was more intriguing than most men. What she felt wasn't just the usual attraction to a handsome face. She might actually be falling for him.

"What a disaster," she breathed.

"What's a disaster, dear?"

Her aunt's voice made her jump. She hadn't realized she had spoken aloud. "Ah, I was just thinking about...the Indian uprising."

Aunt Belle shuddered. "I try *not* to think about it."

Good, Rebecca thought, that meant there was little chance she wanted to *talk* about it. At the same time, she was glad for the interruption. Her thoughts had turned in another crazy direction. She wasn't falling for Clark Forrester. And she would prove it. She would ride up ahead and talk to him and the sergeant about... why, the Indian uprising, of course.

She shifted position in the saddle in anticipation of a short gallop, but that was as far as she went. If she rode anywhere near the lieutenant she would be tempted to tease him. If he so much as spoke to her, she would be running to his tent after supper for that chess game. If he gave her the least encouragement, she'd be begging him to kiss her—probably right in front of Private Powers.

She wasn't falling for him yet, she told herself. The problem was that she *could,* if she wasn't careful.

By evening, when the troop camped a few miles beyond Fort Harker, Rebecca was so agitated even her aunt commented on it. "I imagine it's the coffee, dear," she said. "It's so much stronger than the tea we're used to. Pass it up at supper, and you'll feel better tomorrow."

Rebecca murmured her thanks for the advice. She knew coffee had nothing to do with the way she felt, but if it kept Aunt Belle from inquiring further, she would go along.

She had made a small effort at their noon stop to locate Powers. She had thought she would pass her regrets to Clark through him. She had found herself actually glad when he hadn't turned up immediately. Of course, she had been afraid to seek out Clark in person; she might have relented and told him she was looking forward to the rematch, instead of begging off.

But after the long afternoon, she thought she had figured out her problem. The only reason she was having trouble dismissing him was that he dismissed her so easily. She felt more certain than ever that avoiding Clark was the best policy. She would tell him herself that she would not be playing chess with him. Her mind only half registered the inconsistency of her plan.

While Brooks was setting up their camp, she went in search of Clark's. She found his tent, recognizing it because it was slightly larger than the others, but no one was around. She questioned a soldier camped nearby and learned that the lieutenant and a few men had gone into Fort Harker.

She was irritated with herself as she walked back to the wagon. Of course he would go in and report to the post commander. He would want news of the uprising. There might even be a telegram waiting for him there.

An idea made her outlook brighten. There might be a telegram for her from Father. She could ride in and find out. While she was there, she might see Clark. More foolishness, she realized. She couldn't interrupt the officers' conversation even if she knew the post commander, which she didn't think she did though he probably knew her father. And, she told herself for the millionth time, she was avoiding Clark, except to tell him she wasn't playing chess tonight. If there was a telegram for her, Clark, of course, would see that she got it.

Her agitation had turned to depression by the time she joined her aunt at the camp table. Belle was darning a hole in a stocking, and spoke without looking up. "Where were you off to in such a hurry?"

"Nothing important. Aunt Belle," she continued

with sudden enthusiasm, "do you want to go into town?"

"No."

"But, Aunt Belle, there may be a store—"

"I said no, Rebecca. The town is Ellsworth. I remember General Hale's description, even if you don't. Neither I, nor you, will set foot in that town."

Rebecca fell silent and watched her aunt take tiny even stitches until she thought she would go mad. "Where's Alicia?"

"She's with that driver fellow and his companions learning how to cook over a fire. Foolishness, but it keeps her busy."

Rebecca stared at her aunt's profile. Alicia was out of her mother's sight with not one but four men. And Belle thought cooking was all that was on anybody's mind? Either she was getting used to being around the soldiers, or Alicia had made herself such a pest that Belle was glad to be rid of her. Neither seemed especially likely.

"Where are they?" Rebecca asked, hoping it sounded like a casual question. She realized with a start that she was considering joining them to make sure Alicia was all right. Was she turning into Aunt Belle?

"Right there," Aunt Belle said, pointing with her needle.

They were hidden from Rebecca's view by a tent, but, she realized, not from Belle's. She found herself relieved that things hadn't drifted too far from the familiar.

After dinner, Rebecca mentally prepared herself to visit Clark. She would smile, explain that her aunt needed her to help with some mending, casually wish him a good-night, and leave. Leave him wanting more, she thought with a smile before she could catch herself.

Perhaps she should wait for half an hour or so. That would give him time to miss her, even wonder if she was coming. She pictured him pacing his tent, the chessboard ready and waiting. She smiled to herself, then wanted to smack her forehead. Her brain was still anticipating conquest.

The sooner she saw him the better. Her pulse even leapt at that thought. Maybe it was the coffee, she told herself.

She was about to rise from the chair when her aunt looked up, focusing on something over Rebecca's shoulder. She turned to find Powers coming toward them.

"Ladies," he said politely, doffing his hat.

Rebecca made the introductions. Aunt Belle, obviously not interested in meeting another soldier, returned to her sewing. Already the woman was starting to fit into the military where the officers' families never socialized with enlisted men.

"Miss Huntington," Powers said. "Lieutenant

Forrester sent me back with a message. He's held up at the fort for the evening."

Rebecca stared at him as if the implications of the message were beyond her understanding.

Powers, evidently reading the confusion on her face, added, "He regrets that he will miss the chess game."

Rebecca managed to thank him and wish him good-night.

Aunt Belle's voice seemed to grate against raw nerves. "You had a date to play chess with the lieutenant? That's not only inappropriate, it's foolish. Men aren't interested in women who play men's games. Why your father ever taught you is beyond me."

"Yes, Aunt Belle," Rebecca murmured absently. Clark had broken the date. She was prepared to break it, but *he* had done it first. What could keep him occupied at the fort for so long? Or was that merely an excuse?

And there had been no mention of postponing the game to another night. Was this a rejection? She had no experience with this sort of thing, at least not from this side. She decided she hated it! It was painful. It was humiliating. And she had done it to how many men?

She felt like the earth was about to open up and swallow her. This had been his revenge. She had manipulated her old friend until he ordered Clark to take her with him. She had held the threat of her father's power to get her own way.

So he had charmed her. And dumped her. Only she had been more than charmed. She was on the verge of falling in love.

No, that was foolish, she told herself. She didn't fall in love. And even if he ended the relationship before she could, it didn't really matter. It was bound to happen someday. Besides, she could comfort herself with knowing she had been planning to end it.

Of course, he didn't know that. *He* thought he was putting her in her place. *He* thought she would be hurt. *He* thought she would be humiliated. It was suddenly extremely important that she set him straight.

Powers brought one more message from Clark before the ladies retired. The lieutenant trusted the ladies would stay close to their wagon and take every precaution for their own safety once they left the protection of the fort.

Aunt Belle took that to mean that there were Indians behind every bush and announced her intention to remain inside the wagon at all times. Alicia decided on a return to pants.

Rebecca saw the message in a different light. Clark was requesting that she not ride at the head of the column with him and the sergeant. An insult, she decided, on top of his earlier injury. She went to sleep still wondering what she would do about it.

* * *

Something woke Rebecca after too brief a sleep. She lay still, trying to figure out if she had heard something or if some dream had brought her awake. She *hadn't* dreamed that Clark had tapped on the ambulance and invited her out for a moonlight stroll. *That* notion had been conjured by her fully conscious mind.

She was obsessed. She shifted her position and muffled a groan against her pillow. She should go back to sleep before her fantasies kept her awake all night.

Somehow the night seemed to hang suspended. She held her breath. It was the strangest feeling, as if the air was filled with waiting. She strained her ears for any sound that might have given her the odd impression. She could hear her aunt's soft snoring. Somewhere a cricket chirped.

She had nearly decided her imagination was playing tricks on her, when the back flap of the wagon eased open, spilling moonlight on shiny blond hair. Rebecca watched Alicia ease out of the wagon.

With skill born of practice, Rebecca slipped noiselessly out of her blankets and followed. "Alicia," she hissed the moment the flap had fallen back into place.

Alicia was only a few paces away. She turned, her finger coming quickly to her lips. Rebecca joined her. "You shouldn't be out alone," she whispered.

"I thought you were asleep." Alicia cast a glance over her shoulder.

Until that moment, Rebecca had assumed Alicia needed to relieve herself. Now, with sudden insight, she knew Alicia was sneaking out to meet someone. "Where are you going?" she demanded in as hushed a tone as her fear would permit. It was one thing to go sneaking off herself. It was quite another to find her young cousin doing it.

"To meet Victor. You will cover for me, won't you?"

"Victor? Who's Victor?" Rebecca had stepped closer and took her cousin's hand, hoping to coax Alicia back into the wagon before their conversation woke Aunt Belle.

"Victor Brooks. Our driver."

"Brooks?" Rebecca almost choked on the word. "You can't go off in the middle of the night and meet Brooks."

"And why not? You've done this kind of thing often enough."

Rebecca heard accusation in the whispered words. "But you have to be careful of your choice, Alicia. And Brooks..."

"Rebecca, you're a snob." Alicia pulled her hand out of Rebecca's grasp. "You wouldn't give Brooks a second thought because he's an enlisted man. You didn't even remember his first name."

Rebecca shook her head, wanting to deny the accusation even as she realized there was a grain of truth in it. "Alicia," she began, forcing her voice to remain calm. "Brooks tried to kiss me."

"And your lieutenant didn't?"

Rebecca sighed in exasperation. "That's completely different."

"How is it different? Because it's *me* some man is interested in? Because your lieutenant doesn't want to see you? I think you're jealous."

Rebecca took a step backward. She didn't know what to say to refute the outlandish statement. Alicia took it as an invitation to end the conversation. With a toss of her blond hair, she spun around and hurried away.

Rebecca considered going after her, but what could she say that would mean anything right now? Perhaps she should follow and spy on the couple. She would be close by if things got out of hand. She realized the foolishness of that even as she took the first few steps in the direction her cousin had gone. What she considered out of hand and what Alicia did would likely be two different things. If Brooks actually took liberties, all Alicia had to do was scream and forty or so men would come to her rescue. On the other hand, if he so much as touched her, Rebecca would want to storm forward and drag the girl away.

With a sigh of resignation, Rebecca turned and crept back to the wagon. It wasn't until she was curled up in her bed again that it occurred to her that this entire predicament was her fault.

Chapter Six

Early the next morning, Rebecca walked slowly through the camp. She had to do something to set things right, and she could think of only one way to do it.

Looking back she realized that Alicia actually hadn't been gone from the wagon for very long. At the time, however, it had seemed like hours. Had Alicia worried about her the same way when the situation was reversed?

She shook her head. The circumstances weren't the same. Alicia knew Rebecca could take care of herself. And Rebecca knew Alicia couldn't.

She spotted Clark's tent ahead. He had hung the mirror on a tent post and stood before it mixing soap in a cup. His back was to her, but she easily recognized the breadth of his bare shoulders and the dark hair curling to the base of his neck.

Rebecca eased forward slowly, ignoring a soldier's

apology when he brushed against her as she passed a tent. She was going to do it again. She was going to watch Clark shave. Her stomach shivered with anticipation.

He adjusted the mirror, and she caught the glimpse of his eyes before he turned around. She stood-stock still for a moment. It hadn't occurred to her that he might catch her.

Smiling, she tried to pull herself together. "I didn't want to disturb you," she said.

"That's quite all right. What can I do for you, Rebecca?"

There was the barest pause before he said her name. He set the cup aside and reached for his uniform blouse. Rebecca came forward trying not to look at the broad chest that was quickly disappearing beneath the shirt.

"I need to talk to you," she said.

"Of course. Can I get you a chair?"

"No thanks," she said. "This will only take a moment."

She hoped she was right. She was feeling a need to escape before she gave in to the temptation to test the texture of a day's worth of stubble on his cheek. This was the first time a decision to end a flirtation had resulted in the man in question becoming more attractive. Before, the man's flaws had become more apparent. In Clark's case even his military bearing which had seemed alternately irritating and humorous now seemed endearing.

"Ma'am?"

Rebecca blinked. Lord, she'd been staring. For a second she forgot what she had come to say.

He spoke again. "I hope I didn't worry you and the other ladies with my message last night. I merely wanted to take every precaution for your safety."

"Message?" The only message she remembered was the one canceling their chess game. Then she recalled his warning to stay in camp. "No." She shook her head, hoping to clear it. She had to get this over with. "It's about my cousin. And our driver."

One eyebrow shot up, and she felt herself start to smile. "Yes, it's Alicia this time instead of me."

"What has happened?"

His expression was back to its usual unreadable calm. He could be sympathizing or condemning; she had no way of knowing. She told herself it didn't matter. "Would it be possible to assign us another driver?"

"Of course. But I need to know why."

"He and Alicia have become...too friendly."

"And that bothers you?"

Did she detect the barest note of sarcasm in his voice? She half turned and stepped away from him, her eyes studying the cloudless sky. "I recognize the irony of the situation. But I have reason to be leery of Brooks."

He moved to stand in front of her. There was a hint of concern in his voice as he asked, "What reason?"

"Never mind," she began, finding herself gazing into his gray eyes again. "The point is Alicia doesn't know what she's getting into."

He spoke just above a whisper. "Are you jealous?"

Rebecca sighed, swallowing the humiliation. "Look, I know this is my fault. I'm trying to take responsibility for my actions. I'll talk to Alicia, but I would like to have Brooks farther away from her. Would you arrange that, Lieutenant?"

He nodded. "Sergeant Whiting will be along in a few minutes, and I'll tell him to make the appropriate reassignments."

"Thanks," she murmured, turning quickly away.

She felt the barest touch on her arm. "Rebecca?"

Even before she turned back, his arm had dropped to his side.

"I didn't want to cancel our game last night. I wonder if we could reschedule for this evening."

No. That would be foolish. That would be crazy! She opened her mouth to refuse when she caught a glimpse of vulnerability in his eyes. It startled her into agreeing.

As she headed toward the ambulance, she considered what she had done. In her heart she had wanted to see him again. She had been willing to imagine anything in order to give in. Still, he had asked her. The night before hadn't been the rejection she had imagined.

Unless he was feeling guilty about it. Or thought that was the real reason she had come.

She had never been so confused by a man in her life. She had half a mind to turn around and ask him. "Just what do you mean by dumping me one day and encouraging me the next?" she would ask. "If you are determined to resist my charms why make me want to use them?"

Rebecca stopped suddenly, catching a gasp with her fingertips. She *had* turned around! Or wandered in a circle like some poor soul lost in a blizzard. But now that she was here, she couldn't pull herself away.

His back was bare except for the towel slung across his left shoulder. He leaned toward the mirror, brushed lather on his face, and began to shave. Rebecca watched every flex of his muscles, every efficient motion of his hands. He was halfway through the process when the approach of another soldier brought his head up, and Rebecca's as well.

"Good morning, Sergeant," Clark said, and Rebecca turned and hurried back to the ambulance.

Rebecca spent the morning trying to sort out her feelings. By noon she realized she could no longer deny that she was in love with Clark. She had been so certain that love was simply romantic foolishness.

She had found the perfect alternative: enjoy a man's attention, then move on to another. But she couldn't imagine flirting with another man now. She toyed with the idea of blaming him for ruining her life, but she had a feeling he had saved it instead.

During the noon stop, Rebecca decided she would ride with Clark and the sergeant. Aunt Belle, choosing to continue in her dresses, kept herself hidden away in the wagon, and Alicia, when she was out where Rebecca might have talked to her, sulked beside the new driver. She saw no reason to remain alongside the ambulance and much to tempt her to the front of the line.

The familiar creak of leather and jingle of harnesses was almost hypnotic. Clark suppressed a sigh. Another long day's march with the June sun giving them a taste of what August would be like. It would take three more days to reach Fort Hays. There would be three more evenings to spend with Rebecca before the social life of the fort sent her in pursuit of someone else. He wondered if he could keep her attention for that long. He marveled that he even wanted to, knowing how quickly she would forget him. Instead of admitting that he was better off losing her sooner than later, he felt compelled to spend every possible moment with her, no matter how few.

He found himself wishing for an emergency that would allow his military training to return his familiar control. To have all thought of Rebecca Huntington banished from his mind sounded liberating.

"Miss Huntington."

The sergeant's greeting brought Clark's head around. An emergency all right, just the wrong kind.

Whiting tipped his hat to the young woman as she rode up beside him. "Glad to have your company, ma'am."

"Why, thank you, Mr. Whiting," she said, flashing him a smile.

She hadn't spared a glance at Clark. But then, the sergeant rode between them. Spending the afternoon listening to her flirt with Whiting was going to be worse than missing her.

"Ma'am, if you don't mind," Whiting said, "I'd like you to ride between us. Not meaning to frighten you or anything, but I'd be more comfortable knowing you had that little bit of protection."

He drew his horse around, and they quickly traded places. Clark wasn't sure if Whiting was really being chivalrous or if he was playing matchmaker. He didn't care. She was right where he wanted her. He gave her a polite smile but wondered if his eyes hadn't betrayed his pleasure. Her grin looked almost wicked.

"I trust the new driver is acceptable," he said, hoping to distract her from whatever flirtatious thoughts were circling in her head.

She turned serious immediately. "Yes. Thank you."

The deep concern in her eyes was at least as compelling as a dimpled grin.

"What did you learn at the fort last night?" she asked.

"I did worry you, didn't I? I'm sorry."

She shook her head. "I'd rather be a little worried and safe than ignorant of the danger. What did you learn?"

Clark considered how much he should tell her. She wouldn't settle for a few generalities; the determination in her eyes told him that. Still, she was a woman.

"Every available soldier is out searching for the hostiles."

"And they haven't so much as seen them, have they?"

He shifted uncomfortably. "No, ma'am."

A curl blew across her cheek, and she tucked it behind her ear. "So the Cheyenne continue to raid. But what can anyone expect? Hancock burned their homes."

"It's not only the Cheyenne who are raiding."

She looked at him sharply, and he wondered why he was telling her this. Was he so desperate to keep her attention? Or did those trusting eyes simply demand the truth? "Kiowa. Even some Sioux."

"Raiding in sympathy?"

Clark shook his head. "Perhaps. More likely they've just found the excuse they've been waiting for."

"But with so many soldiers on patrol wouldn't that be dangerous?"

"It hasn't been so far."

She studied him thoughtfully as she said, "You don't think the troops will be successful?"

He hesitated a moment before answering softly, "I think the hostiles will watch the soldiers and wait for them to make a mistake. They'll attack only if they know they can win. They will continue raiding and avoiding the army until winter. Then they'll hole up somewhere until spring when it'll start all over again."

"What would you do?" It was almost a whisper.

"I'll follow orders."

"That's not what I asked."

He watched her search his eyes for a moment before he spoke. "What I would do, is immaterial."

"That's silly."

Clark couldn't resist a mirthless laugh. "I'm afraid the opposite is true. It's silly to devise a plan I have no power to carry out."

She was still eyeing him speculatively as if she read more on his face than he thought he had given away. "You have an opinion," she said.

He shook his head and knew she didn't believe

him. "You have one, I would imagine. How would you approach the situation?"

She looked slightly irked to have the tables turned on her. He watched her chew her lip as she considered how to answer. It was moist and pink when she released it. He had to turn away for fear he would be so fascinated by the sight that he wouldn't hear what she said. He didn't want to be accused a second time of not respecting her.

"The Indians have been wronged," she began. "Their homes should be replaced."

"And their depredations forgiven?" He turned back toward her. She was beautiful. Her cheeks and lips seemed to glow in the sunlight. Her eyes, shaded by the hat, seemed dark with mystery.

"This is war, Lieutenant. When it ends the soldiers are usually forgiven."

"And sometimes the losing generals are hanged." He immediately wished he hadn't said it. But he had, and he couldn't turn away. "Besides," he added softly, "I don't believe the settlers and railroad workers knew they were at war."

After a long moment she whispered, "Maybe they should hang Hancock."

The comment startled a laugh out of him. "Forgive me, ma'am, but being an officer myself I don't believe I'd like the precedent."

"I'm serious, Clark. If the government had hanged

Chivington after Sand Creek, none of this would be happening now.''

"That's a bit of a leap."

She shook her head and turned away.

Clark let his eyes scan the horizon. It was easy to get caught up in conversation with Rebecca and forget the immediate danger. What he had learned at the fort and not told her included raids within a few miles of the trail they followed now.

"If you'll excuse me, ma'am," Whiting said. "I couldn't help overhearing your conversation with the lieutenant here, and I gotta say giving these renegades their homes back wouldn't stop the raids."

"What do you mean?"

Clark felt his jaw muscles tighten when she turned toward the sergeant. It was one thing for him to disagree with her. It was quite another for someone else to. He felt an irrational desire to defend her argument.

"Well," Whiting said, "we gotta have a few victories, inflict a little pain. See, they'd rather be raiding than living peacefully in the first place. They got no real incentive to quit."

"I can't believe that."

Whiting responded kindly, "No, ma'am, I don't suppose you can."

Clark wanted to see Rebecca's reaction to her exchange with the sergeant, but she didn't turn back in his direction for some time. When she did, her usual good nature had returned. They rode in contemplative silence for most of the afternoon. What little conversation they shared concerned trivial matters. Clark found the situation surprisingly comfortable. Odd to discover now that he liked the girl.

When it was getting close to time to make camp, Rebecca cast Clark a teasing smile and asked Whiting if he had heard about the chess game of two nights before.

"It's common knowledge around camp, ma'am," he answered. "You beat our lieutenant here. I'm proud of you, but not all the fellas feel the same."

She glanced at Clark again, this time her eyes were full of dismay. Evidently she didn't realize the sergeant was teasing.

"There's a rematch scheduled for this evening," Clark said, bringing her attention back to him. "I will attempt to exonerate myself." He gave her a smile and watched her relax.

"I'm glad to hear that, sir," Whiting said. "I'm afraid most of the boys feel the honor of all men is at stake."

"I'll have to keep my wits about me," Clark added softly.

Rebecca was frustrated by even the slightest delay that evening. It wasn't that she hated to keep a man waiting; that had never seemed like a bad strategy. She was simply impatient to be with Clark again as soon as possible.

While Aunt Belle was not happy to learn of her plans for the evening, Alicia seemed positively livid. She expressed her resentment by refusing to speak to Rebecca at all. Rebecca could hardly blame her. Alicia wanted to spend time with Brooks the way Rebecca would with Clark. There was a world of difference between the two men, but Rebecca didn't know how to explain that to her cousin. Besides, Alicia was in no mood to listen to anything right now.

Finally, after a tense meal served by strangers, Rebecca made her way to the lieutenant's tent. Powers was waiting outside to usher her in. "Lieutenant Forrester, your guest is here," he said, as if the tent were some huge hall in which her arrival might pass unnoticed.

Clark closed a journal and stood, indicating the chair across from him with the an outstretched hand. The chess game was already arranged on the camp desk.

"Can I get you some coffee, ma'am?" Powers asked.

"No, thank you." Rebecca smiled at Powers as she sank into the chair, then turned her attention to Clark. He spared Powers a glance as he resumed his seat, checking perhaps to see that the man didn't leave.

"I believe it's your turn to play first," she said.

Clark nodded. "I don't suppose it would be wise for me to turn down even the slightest advantage."

They each played several turns in near silence, positioning their pieces for their own strategies. Rebecca knew that she had won so handily before because she had managed to keep Clark distracted. She was going to have to work harder at it tonight.

"Clark," she said after making a particularly careful move. "Would you call yourself a Galvanized Yankee?"

An eyebrow quirked up at the question. She was delighted.

"I don't," he said. "But some folks back home do, I suppose."

"What do you mean?"

Clark studied the board for a moment, then evidently decided not to risk a move at the moment. "I was just out of West Point when the war began. I was a second lieutenant in the United States Army. I had no intention of fighting against my own country. But I didn't want to fight against my own state, my own neighbors, either. I requested service in the West.

"Since I wear the blue uniform, I'm not especially welcome back home. Any southerner who fought for the north might be called a Galvanized Yankee, among other things. Out here it usually refers to the Confederate soldiers who were recruited into the army of the West from the northern prisons."

She was delighted to learn some of his history, but he wasn't playing. "So you came west about the time

I was sent east," she said, smiling. "It seems we just missed each other."

"I assure you, Miss Huntington," his voice dropped to a seductive murmur, "if I had so much as passed by you on my trip west, I would remember."

Oh, my. Now who was distracting whom? While she sat staring at him, he had the audacity to lower his eyes to the board. She tried to do the same. She couldn't make sense of her own pieces, let alone his. Hadn't she had a plan? Hadn't she thought a few minutes ago that she knew his?

Maybe he was playing two games. She had to get the upper hand in at least one of them. Chess was safer. But less interesting.

She leaned slightly toward the bent head. "What a romantic thought, Lieutenant," she said just above a whisper. "The young soldier's glimpse of a beautiful woman sustains him through six arduous years on the plains."

He raised his head, their faces mere inches apart. "It didn't happen. Sorry." He drew a little closer, and her breath caught in her throat. He whispered, "Your play."

Rebecca sat back and laughed. She tried to concentrate on the board, but her eyes kept wandering back to his face. He wore his usual placid expression except his eyes fairly danced. He had enjoyed teasing her. Perhaps her best bet was to turn him serious again. But first she would play.

She studied the board and discovered he had put her queen in danger. She used it to jump his offending knight and started a veritable bloodbath. First he jumped her queen. Then her half-finished strategy fell apart as she took every opportunity to decimate his ranks. He responded in kind at nearly every turn.

Just as quickly it was over. Rebecca looked down at the few pieces scattered across the board. The kings, of course, had been protected but not much else. "What wanton destruction," she muttered.

He laughed, and she looked up quickly to see his face, glad she hadn't missed what she suspected was a rare display of pleasure.

"You could concede now," he said. "I see no way you can win."

"I see no way you can win, either," she retorted.

"Ah, but I have both a bishop and a castle. I can corner your king."

"But I have my castle to stave off your pieces and two pawns. I could get my queen back."

He shook his head. "They'd never make it all the way down here."

"We could call it a stalemate."

He opened his mouth as if to disagree, then laughed again. Rebecca loved the sound. She vowed to make him laugh as often as possible.

"Stalemate it is," he said graciously. He came to

his feet and offered her his hand as she rose. "Would you consent to a game again tomorrow night? I hold out hope of winning at least once."

Rebecca stood beside him, surprised but pleased that he hadn't released her hand. "Perhaps we should switch to poker," she suggested and smiled when his eyebrow shot upward.

"I'm afraid that could prove expensive. Mr. Powers," he said, turning toward the striker as he tucked Rebecca's hand in his elbow. "That will be all. I'll see Miss Huntington back to her wagon."

They followed Powers out of the tent and started slowly toward the ambulance. The camp was not entirely quiet but the voices and stirrings were muffled and soft. Crickets and frogs provided a discordant lullaby.

"Have you regretted it?" Rebecca asked softly. "Choosing the West, I mean?"

"No. It is part of the reason I'm only a first lieutenant, though. My superiors, for the most part, distinguished themselves during the war between the states. This war out here isn't considered as noble a cause."

"Are you ambitious, Clark?"

"I used to think I was. Advancement now depends on someone's retirement or death. Few men have saved for the former, and I don't like to think I'd wish the latter on anyone. I'm fairly content as things are."

"Fairly?"

"Especially now."

She lifted her face up to his, hoping he would explain. No, hoping something else.

He stopped walking and turned toward her. "A beautiful woman to walk beside me in the moonlight, what more can I ask?"

She leaned toward him, letting her hands rest delicately on his forearms. "I'd ask for a kiss," she whispered.

He made no move toward her. It was hard to see his expression in the dim light. "Miss Huntington," he said softly, "you're out to break my heart."

He stepped aside and gently led her onward. Rebecca found herself trembling. She hadn't realized until this moment how very much she had wanted that kiss. She practically leaned against his strong arm for support, but the heat of his body only added to the trembling.

Near the wagon, he stopped and freed himself from her grasp, squeezing her hand slightly before he let it go. "Good night," he whispered near her ear and slipped away.

She stood looking after him until he was swallowed by the shadows. He didn't go back the way he had come, leaving the impression that he was merely dropping her off on his way someplace else. She didn't like the feeling.

She considered following him to see where he was

going. Then a thought brought a smile to her lips. He was taking a long walk to cool his blood before trying to sleep.

It wasn't until later, when she had gone to bed that she thought about his comment. He had said she was out to break his heart. It wasn't true. She wanted to steal it and keep it and give her own in return. Could his comment have been a gentleman's way of turning aside unwanted advances?

She closed her eyes against the sudden pain. He had been more than charming tonight. He had flirted with her. He had dropped his voice to a timbre that seemed to resonate with her blood. And she had *asked* for a kiss. She had been thoroughly dazzled. She had been right when she told Alicia it was a little like being burned.

Perhaps he had gotten revenge.

Chapter Seven

To help shake off the lethargy left from a nearly sleepless night, Rebecca took a brisk walk around camp after breakfast. It was fate or luck or coincidence that brought her near Clark's tent just as he began to shave. There was no design, conscious or subconscious that brought her there, or so she told herself. She had no explanation for why she stayed to watch.

As she hurried to saddle her horse, her pulse still racing with guilty pleasure, she decided her only hope of ever facing Clark again was to pretend she was completely unaffected by last evening's events. She had been merely teasing, as had he. His kiss would have meant nothing, therefore she wasn't disappointed that he had refused.

It all seemed perfectly clear to her until she rode toward the front. She drew back on the reins to watch the lines being formed. Whiting called the orders and

Clark surveyed the troops. He looked wonderful. Tall and straight in the saddle. Calm yet alert. She was sure even a person unfamiliar with uniforms would see instantly that he was in charge.

Totally in charge.

Where did she ever get the idea that she had dazzled him? Even on the train he had been in control. She was a diversion, as men had always been to her. In spite of his words, his heart was in no danger. In fact, it had barely been touched.

A voice in her head argued that it wasn't so. She had seen his eyes grow warm at the sight of her, had heard desire color his voice. But couldn't she pretend these things as well? Hadn't she counted them among her weapons?

Steeling herself, she kneed her mount forward. Clark gave her a nod in greeting, but instead of turning his attention back to the troops, he let his eyes linger on her.

She forced a broad smile. "Good morning, Lieutenant. It looks like it's going to be another lovely day."

"It does now."

Oh, he was good. He said it without the barest trace of a smile. One could easily believe him sincere. But of course it was part of the game. Her only defense was to turn up her own charm.

She tried to brighten her smile. "So sweet of you to make me feel welcome." She had let a trace of a southern accent creep into her speech, hoping it annoyed him. The game wasn't as fun when she knew he played it too.

In a few minutes the line started forward with her once again riding between Clark and Whiting. She was too unhappy to care to talk and left it to the men to initiate any conversation. Though she tried to respond pleasantly and show an interest in what was said, they may have found her attitude discouraging. Several times they lapsed into long silences.

At noon she joined her aunt and cousin at the wagon and suffered the former's displeasure and the latter's resentment while she ate. Still it would have been easier to stay beside the ambulance for the afternoon's march than to rejoin Clark and pretend to be enchanting. But she couldn't. Her pride demanded that she keep up the pretense.

It was during one of the now familiar silences that Whiting spotted the smoke. Rebecca turned quickly in the direction he pointed. It was a mercifully still day, at least for Kansas, and there was little danger of the fire spreading. But it seemed ominous nonetheless.

"What do you think it is?" she asked, turning to Clark. The way he watched the trail ahead made her wonder if he had noticed the smoke sometime earlier.

"I don't want to guess. We'll find out when we get closer."

It seemed forever before he called a halt. "Sergeant, take four men and scout the perimeter. Send four with me. Everyone else is to stay close and remain alert." He turned to Rebecca. "Go back to the wagon."

He didn't wait for Whiting to relay the orders, but rode toward what was clearly the smoldering remains of a building. Four soldiers quickly caught up with him.

Whiting had his men selected but paused at Rebecca's side. "You should go back like he said."

Rebecca nodded. "Of course." But she sat staring after Clark and the others as Whiting turned away.

Had there been an Indian attack? Clark's orders indicated that was his suspicion. But perhaps someone's carelessness had caused their cabin to burn. An upset lamp. A spark from the chimney landing on a wood-shingled roof. She had to know.

A closer look revealed the building to be a sod house with its roof completely caved in. Thin streams of smoke curled up from two or three separate spots inside. Tools and household goods were scattered around the yard.

She drew rein as Clark came around the side of the building. He glanced at her before speaking to the men. "Get shovels from the supply wagon and see if you can put the last of the fire out. There are bodies inside that should be buried."

She sat frozen as he walked toward her. The

breeze's soft caress and a quail's whistle seemed out of place in the face of this stark destruction.

"You don't follow orders well, do you?" He caught her horse's chin strap when it would have sidestepped away from him.

"What happened here?"

He glanced over his shoulder before he spoke. "I can't be certain, but I know those people did not die in the fire."

Rebecca swung to the ground, feeling a need to be moving, doing something.

"You should go back," he said gently. He took the last step that separated them and raised a hand to touch her arm. She wondered if she had swayed. She hoped not.

"I want to help," she said.

A slight smile touched his lips. "Are you good with a shovel?"

She lowered her eyes. There had to be something she could do. "I could collect their personal effects to send to the next of kin."

He shook his head. "You won't find much in there."

"I can try."

He turned away to study the building for a moment before he answered. "Let me hear Sergeant Whiting's report so I know if there's any further danger. Then, once we get the bodies out, you can go in."

"You don't have to protect me. I've seen death before."

His eyes met hers. What she saw stirring in their depths made her tremble. "Not like this," he said before he turned away.

Rebecca stayed beside her horse at the edge of the yard watching. Whiting rode in and reported that he had seen the trail of a band of Indians, twenty or more, but they were long gone. The four men with him joined the burial detail, and Clark sent Whiting back to the caravan to set up camp and post guards. When the bodies were wrapped in blankets and lifted from the rubble, Clark returned to Rebecca's side.

"You can go in, but I want you to be careful. I think the walls will stand, but there could be live coals anywhere."

She nodded her understanding and started forward, absently handing the reins to Clark. She heard Clark call to one of the soldiers but had no curiosity about his purpose. The smell of ashes and smoke seemed to reach out to her, and she had to struggle not to turn away. The smallest memento could mean so much to a brother or sister or parent.

She stepped through the narrow doorway and her heart sank. Clark had been right. The destruction appeared to be nearly complete. Everything was black and ugly and deformed.

Before she could do more than look around in bewilderment, she felt a presence behind her. She turned to find Clark. She almost hoped he had changed his mind and had come to send her back to the wagon.

"Take your pick," he said. One hand held a hoe, the other the long handle of a broken garden tool. Until that moment, she hadn't noticed that he was holding anything. She accepted the handle with a smile of gratitude.

"I think the fire was concentrated over there," he said, tipping his head toward his left. "Our best chance of finding anything will probably be here."

He stepped around her and used the hoe to turn over chunks of the burned roof.

"You don't need to help me," she said, moving quickly to begin her own search.

"The men have the burials well under control, and I can trust Whiting to take care of the camp. But I can't bear to think of you in here by yourself."

A hint of color under the ashes made her kneel to dig more carefully. "Well," she said as she worked, "I'm grateful for the company."

"Getting a little spooked, were you?" He was kneeling close beside her.

"More discouraged, I think." She uncovered a broken piece of china, intricately painted and probably treasured. Even if she found the other pieces, they couldn't be pieced together. It seemed a sad memento.

"Look at this." He held something toward her between gloved fingers. "It's hot," he warned when she reached for it. With his other hand he laid it in his palm. It was a medal of some kind. Scraps of charred cloth showed where a ribbon had burned away.

"A soldier?"

Clark nodded. "During the war, I would imagine. Neighbors will know who lived here."

He said something more as he resumed his search but Rebecca didn't hear him. She had tossed aside a chunk of wood that had probably been furniture and stared into the face of a small rag doll. Part of her hair and dress had been singed and the stitched smile and eyes were streaked with soot.

Rebecca lifted it reverently. She had to swallow twice before she could speak. "Was one of the bodies a child?"

"Yes." Clark's whisper caressed her cheek. He had moved very close to her. She appreciated the gesture, but his nearness tempted her to give in to the threatening tears and seek comfort in his arms.

She set the doll aside and hastily resumed her efforts. At least the child wasn't a captive, she told herself. Unless the doll belonged to a sister of the child the soldiers were burying. She shook off the thought. As Clark had said, the neighbors would know.

She had no idea how much time had passed when

she felt Clark catch her arm. As she turned toward him she realized he had been calling her name.

"I don't think we'll find much else," he said gently. He pointed to the pitiful pile of trinkets at their feet. "These few things will bring the family some comfort."

"Will they?"

He nodded his assurance. She let the handle slip from her hand to join the debris at her feet. Clark tried to lead her forward but she slipped from his grasp, bending to lift the doll. Leaving the rest for Clark to gather she stumbled out of the sod house. Nearby the soldiers were finishing the burials. It was easy to tell which grave was the child's. The mound of dirt was barely four feet long. Against the rocks that had been stacked to form a crude headstone, Rebecca gently placed the doll.

Clark strolled toward his tent. It wasn't full dark but already the camp was quieting down. In spite of the early stop, there had been very little commotion. Most of the soldiers were subdued by what they had seen.

He took a deep breath, wishing he was farther away from the cook fires. He wore clean civilian clothes and his body was clean, or at least as clean as he could make it in the little trickle of the creek, but he didn't think he would ever get the stench of charred wood and burned bodies out of his nose.

Near his tent, he checked the clothesline Powers had rigged to dry his uniform and determined it was in no danger of toppling over. A soft inviting light shone through the tent opening. Powers again, he supposed.

He stepped inside his tent and was brought up short. "Rebecca. I didn't expect to see you tonight."

A slight smile touched her lips. "You're out of uniform, Lieutenant."

"So are you, soldier."

She ran her hands down the sides of her dark brown dress, probably chosen to be less visible at night. "It's an odd time, I know, to go back to dresses, but my uniform was filthy."

"Mine was as well." He watched her look nervously around the tent. "Rebecca, are you all right?"

She took a step toward him. "I've put them in danger, haven't I? Aunt Belle and Alicia? Because I was so impatient to get home to Father."

He hated to see her distressed. He wanted to wrap her in his arms, but he would probably gain more comfort than she. "Perhaps, Rebecca," he began, searching for words, "but there are dangers everywhere. Trains derail. Carriages run over people. No place is completely safe."

"But those are accidents. I brushed off reasonable warnings."

He moved toward her, meaning to draw her closer. It occurred to him suddenly that they were alone.

Any number of men might have seen them both enter the tent. Their silhouettes could even now be visible through the canvas. "Let me walk you back," he said.

"Clark." Her tone was a protest.

"I'm not dismissing you, I'm protecting you." He all but dragged her out of the tent then set a leisurely pace toward the ambulance. "Rebecca," he said softly, "none of us knew how this would escalate. Back at Fort Riley, we made our decisions based on the information we had at the time."

"I didn't."

Clark smiled down at her. "Well, I did."

She shook her head, her eyes on the ground. "You thought I was blackmailing you. If you didn't agree to take me, I'd tell the general some outrageous version of what happened on the train."

"Would you have?"

She looked up at him sharply and seemed annoyed by his smile. "Of course not."

"I'll admit that the thought did cross my mind. But if I had known the kind of danger we might be in, I would never have traded your safety for my career."

"You would have faced a court-martial rather than follow a direct order to take me?"

His hand slid against her cheek and under her short curly hair almost of its own volition. "If I had thought the danger was severe, yes. I'm not convinced even now that we are in that kind of danger. It's unlikely that the hostiles will attack soldiers, though they may try to run off our horses. There are guards posted and we are well-armed. And we're only a day and a half from Fort Hays.''

She sighed and closed her eyes. The temptation to kiss her was so great he pulled his hand back and stepped away from her. Almost certainly someone was watching them.

He thought he read disappointment in her eyes but knew he could be imagining it. Her next words didn't indicate that she missed his touch.

''I keep thinking about that child.''

He nodded. ''It's sad. And it sounds cold, but life goes on.''

''For the rest of us.''

He ignored the bitterness in her voice. ''Exactly,'' he said. ''If we let ourselves be overwhelmed by the deaths around us, our lives are ruined as well.''

He let her come to terms with what he had said. When she gave him a slight nod, he took her arm and turned her toward the ambulance again. ''Go back and convince your aunt and cousin that they'll live to see Fort Hays,'' he said. ''And tomorrow night, come play chess with me. One last time.''

He watched her walk the short distance to the ambulance before he turned away.

Alicia crept quietly out of the wagon. She moved into the shadow of a nearby tent and crouched low, waiting to see if she had awakened Rebecca. If her cousin followed her this time, she wouldn't tell her where she was going.

Finally, when she was sure she had waited long enough, she rose and hurried to the place Victor had indicated for them to meet. Victor was to be on guard duty there, and no one else should be nearby.

She found her heart pounding as she made her way in the moonlight. She knew it was less her desire to be with Victor than it was the excitement and fear of disobeying.

The image of Rebecca and her lieutenant standing together earlier that evening was burned in her brain. He had touched her cheek tenderly, and Alicia had been sure he would kiss her. But he hadn't. They had spoken only a moment before she left him. Alicia had watched his face as Rebecca walked away. If a man ever looked at *her* with that kind of longing she would cherish him forever. Rebecca, however, was only playing.

Alicia didn't fool herself into thinking that Victor was her perfect love. But he was the first man who had shown more than passing interest, and she still stung from Rebecca's efforts to keep them apart.

She reached the spot where she was to meet Victor, but he was nowhere in sight. The tree-lined creek was a short distance away. Perhaps he was hiding there. Not daring to call his name for fear of alerting someone else, she made her way carefully toward the shadows of the trees.

A hand grabbed her arm and yanked her into the darkness. Another hand muffled her scream. She found herself pressed against a rough tree trunk, images of being scalped swimming in her head.

"I wasn't sure you'd come."

Alicia relaxed a little as she recognized Victor's voice. His hold on her loosened, and he eased his hand from her mouth.

"You frightened me," she whispered.

"I'm sorry," he rasped near her ear, "but we have to be careful. They would ruin everything for us if they found out."

"They?" She wished he would step away. He was so close she was having trouble breathing.

"Your snob of a cousin and Dixie Boy. But they can't keep us from loving each other."

Alicia pressed her hand against his chest, hoping to gain a little space. "Victor, I don't—"

He didn't let her finish. His mouth came down on hers, pressing her against the tree. Tears stung her eyes as the rough bark gouged the back of her head. His mouth on hers made her feel smothered, choked. With all her strength she pressed against his chest. He broke the kiss but gave her only inches in which to gasp for air.

"What's the matter with you?" he growled.

"You hurt me," she said, testing the back of her head with her fingers.

"Well, I'm sorry, but I don't have a tent to myself and a nice soft cot like Dixie Boy." His voice dropped to a suggestive whisper. "We can make do in the grass, sweetheart."

"No!" It came out more loudly than she had intended, and he clamped his hand over her mouth again.

"What do you mean, no?" he hissed. "You came here to meet me. Are you going to pretend you didn't know what I wanted?"

She shook her head and he lifted his hand. "I didn't. I didn't understand. I thought…"

She felt stupid. Stupid and afraid. Rebecca had tried to warn her. Why hadn't she listened? "Please. Let me go back."

"Oh, I'll let you go back, you worthless little tease. But don't think I'll forget this. You're just like her, aren't you? Too good to scratch the itch of a man like me." She tried to turn her face away but he caught her chin, holding her head still as he spoke into her ear. "I'll let you in on a little secret. Under that fancy uniform, an officer ain't no different from me."

He let her go then, shoving her out into the moonlight. She fell to her knees, scraping her hand as she caught herself. Afraid he might change his mind, she scrambled to her feet and ran toward the wagon. Well into the cluster of tents she paused to catch her breath and realized she was sobbing. She couldn't sneak back into the wagon until she had control of herself. She brushed at her wet cheeks and tried to slow her breathing. She imagined herself standing there struggling with her tears the rest of the night.

Rebecca shook away the last of a troubling dream and sat up in her bed. Aunt Belle's light snore was oddly comforting. After several nights in the wagon she had become used to the sound of the others' breathing. It took her only a moment to know that Alicia was gone.

Her stomach churning, she thrust her feet into her shoes and grabbed her brown dress, slipping it over her chemise and buttoning it only after she had climbed from the wagon. Where should she begin to look for Alicia?

She considered waking Clark but it seemed a drastic step when she didn't know how long Alicia had been gone or that it wasn't an innocent visit to the trees to relieve herself. Then she worried that her cousin might be suffering some digestive complaint.

She tried to dismiss the thought. Before she panicked she should make sure the girl wasn't nearby, perhaps having trouble sleeping. She started a slow circle around the ambulance, carefully scanning the shadowy camp.

Halfway around the wagon, she saw the moon

catch the pale hair, making it almost shine. Alicia seemed to be simply standing alone, and Rebecca nearly called out to her, then thought better of it in the sleeping camp.

She started toward the figure, having to shuffle in her untied shoes. "Alicia," she whispered.

Alicia didn't respond, but Rebecca saw her shoulders shake. In a moment she was by her side. "Alicia," she whispered again, touching a shoulder.

Alicia jumped. "Rebecca," she whispered, brushing away tears. "What are you doing out here?"

"I woke up and found you gone. What are you doing?"

"Me?" She cleared her throat. "I got up to...well, you know, and on my way back I fell. See? My dress is torn and I cut my hand."

Rebecca stepped closer, wrapping an arm around her cousin's narrow shoulders. "So you were standing here crying?"

Alicia turned away. "I know it sounds silly, but I was embarrassed. I didn't want to get into the wagon crying like a baby."

"Are you all right now?"

Alicia took a deep breath. It was only slightly shaky. "I think so."

They started back toward the wagon together. Rebecca asked, "Are you feeling all right? You didn't need to go because you were sick, did you?"

Alicia shook her head. "No. I just waited until dark because there's no privacy out here."

Rebecca wasn't entirely satisfied, but she didn't ask any more questions. She helped Alicia into the wagon and slipped in after her. They both undressed and returned to their beds as quietly as possible, listening all the while to Aunt Belle's steady snore.

As she waited for sleep, Rebecca tried to remember every detail of her exchange with her cousin. The story seemed plausible enough, but odd at the same time. She had never known Alicia to give way so easily to tears.

Rebecca didn't think Alicia seemed like her old self the next day. Of course Aunt Belle's scolding for the torn dress could have been partially responsible. Still, she seemed nervous, and Rebecca couldn't help but believe that something had frightened her the night before. She had a suspicion that the something was Victor Brooks.

Even before Rebecca finished breakfast, she knew she would be riding next to the ambulance, if for no other reason than to keep Aunt Belle from adding to Alicia's distress. The day before, her biggest concern had been to make sure Clark thought his flirting had been ineffective. After the burned cabin and Alicia's tears, it seemed so trivial.

Promising her aunt that she would be back quickly, she headed for Clark's tent. She found herself smiling. If Clark was shaving this time, she would march right in and interrupt him. Surely it wouldn't be as embarrassing as she had once supposed.

Her timing was perfect. He dropped the brush in the cup and set it aside, lifting the razor. Now, she told herself, before he actually begins, before she ran the risk of startling him and he cuts himself.

But her feet were rooted to the spot. It was simply too intriguing to watch him scrape the soap away from that strong, lean jaw. It wouldn't take him very long, she reminded herself. It was more polite to wait. And watch? Well, maybe polite wasn't the right word.

She watched each stroke, each flex of his shoulders. When he laid aside the razor and bent to rinse his face in a basin of water, she started forward. She tried to walk purposefully, as if she had only just arrived. She hoped the heat she felt on her face didn't leave a visible stain.

"Good morning, Miss Huntington," he said as he brought a towel to his face.

He hadn't turned. "How did you know it was me?" she asked, feeling her cheeks grow warmer still.

"I recognized your step." He placed the towel beside the cup and razor and reached for his shirt. "What can I do for you?"

Rebecca tried to keep her eyes on his face. It shouldn't have been difficult, she loved his face. But she was curious about the rest, and he didn't seem in any hurry to get the shirt buttoned.

"Rebecca?"

She shook herself. "I wanted to tell you I'll be riding near the wagon today."

"You might be safer there."

She smiled. "It wasn't my safety I was thinking of." What exactly should she say about Alicia? She didn't want to jump to conclusions, yet it seemed only right to say something. Everything that happened in the caravan concerned him. His voice brought her out of her contemplation.

"Tired of my company?"

She laughed. "Of course not."

Maybe that was a little more honest than she should have been. She went on hastily, "Alicia took a scare last night. I don't know exactly what happened, perhaps nothing, but she seems a little nervous and preoccupied this morning. I thought I'd ride with her and try to keep her distracted."

He nodded slowly. "I hope she has recovered enough by evening that you don't have to miss our game."

She grinned. "I'll bring her along, if I have to. I wouldn't want to miss another chance to...threaten your honor."

With a toss of her curls she turned back toward her wagon. That last comment had been way too provocative, and she knew it. But this was Lieutenant Forrester she was talking to, and she couldn't help but wish he was a little less concerned about propriety.

Chapter Eight

Rebecca didn't really consider taking Alicia with
her. The girl seemed better by evening, but even if
she had been a weeping wreck Rebecca would have
left her to her mother.

She started toward the lieutenant's tent a little later
than usual, wishing she could be wearing her red
dress. It wouldn't have been a good idea. Several of
the soldiers had reported seeing Indians during the
day. Though the young recruits were probably jump-
ing at shadows, there was still a chance that they
were being watched. Whether a woman in the caravan would really make any difference or not, was
another question.

Yet, Rebecca had promised to look like a soldier,
not a potential hostage, and she would keep her
promise.

Besides, the red dress didn't have a pocket.

Over the course of the day, her mind had worked

on several entertaining schemes before settling on one. The plan was beautiful in its simplicity.

Powers was waiting as she expected and ushered her in much as he had before. Clark had been sitting on his cot, writing in a journal. He stood, setting the book aside, as she entered.

"How is your cousin?" he asked.

"Better, I think." She should have expected the question, but his unfailing concern for others often took her by surprise.

"And you, Rebecca?" His softened tone made her realize he was thinking of her visit the evening before, the cabin, the child, as well as Alicia.

She smiled. "I'm fine."

"I'm glad." He motioned toward the table. "Shall we?"

The chessboard was tempting, but she had other plans. "Of course," she said, smiling. As she moved toward the waiting chair, she thrust her hands deep into her pockets in what she hoped looked like a casual gesture.

She stopped suddenly. "Oh, no! My aunt's thimble." She drew it out, looking at it in feigned surprise. "She was asking for it just this evening. I must have put it in my pocket the last time I borrowed it."

She turned toward Powers waiting near the doorway. She hoped she was putting just the right amount of dismay in her voice. "She planned to do some mending tonight. She'll cut her poor fingers to pieces without her thimble. Could you take it to her?"

Powers' eyes were on her, his hand automatically reaching for the object she thrust toward him. She put all the pleading and worry she could into her eyes and stepped a little closer than was necessary. As long as he didn't look to Clark for confirmation of the order, this might work. "I'd be so grateful," she murmured.

"Yes, ma'am," he said, slipping out of the tent.

Rebecca sighed with relief. She turned to find Clark staring at her, his mouth open in soundless protest.

She grinned and shrugged.

"Young lady, I have gone to considerable trouble to see that we were never alone."

He seemed mystified by her behavior. She decided to enlighten him. "Sir, I just went to considerable trouble to see that we *are* alone."

He blinked. "Dare I ask to what purpose?"

The bafflement in his expression made her laugh. She grew serious as she moved toward him. "Yesterday I realized how uncertain life is. Clark, we tease and flirt and play games. Somehow honesty gets lost in the process."

He glanced significantly toward the empty doorway. "You're going to talk to me about honesty?"

She had to laugh again. "Honesty in our relationship, at least."

He took a deep breath. "I've found that in relationships, particularly with women, honesty can be risky."

She stood directly before him now. "Clark," she whispered, "I'm ready for some risk."

She wrapped her arms around his neck and used his strong shoulders to pull herself upward. She brought her lips to his but paused just short of touching them. She gave him the space of three heartbeats to claim her lips. He didn't.

She didn't let it bother her. Slowly and deliberately, she took the initiative. She savored the soft warmth against her sensitive lips, the heat of his body, the smell of the Kansas prairie that clung to his hair. He wasn't returning the kiss, but she felt his response in the tension of his shoulders, in his quickening heartbeat.

The tip of her tongue tasted his lips, and she found herself engulfed in sensations. His arms drew her flush against his frame, heating her blood to a weakening degree. His tongue mated with hers, eliciting a moan that seemed to come straight from her soul.

Her breasts, flattened against his hard chest, swelled and ached, not in resistance to the harsh treatment, but as if they craved closer contact.

Her mind was reeling when he raised his head. She tried to open her eyes but her lids merely fluttered lazily. She would have protested if his arms had loosened even a fraction, but they held her as fast as ever.

"This is crazy," he murmured.

She would have agreed. In fact she tried to. All that made it past her lips was a sigh.

She thought she heard—or felt—him chuckle. She opened her eyes to find him smiling at her. The smile faded quickly as he lowered his lips back to hers.

His kiss was both sweet surrender and restrained passion. The gentle joining of their lips seemed to expose his heart to hers and made her believe in love. Yet, even as she gloried in this new knowledge, he was gently releasing her.

In a moment she stood before him, her breath still coming in quick painful bursts, her heart still beating erratically. His hands on her shoulders supported her as the haze of passion left her brain.

He was smiling gently. "I have to take you back."

She shook her head but knew he wouldn't hear her arguments.

"This is neither the time nor the place."

Realization hit her, helping to cool her blood. Powers' imminent return, the possibility of an Indian attack, Clark's career, and even her own reputation flashed through her mind. Her clever idea to steal another kiss had gotten way out of hand.

She took a deep breath and let it out slowly, then tossed him a rueful smile. "Do you suppose we should be playing chess when Powers returns?"

Clark shook his head. "How long does it take to return a thimble? Powers may well have been back.

It's hard to tell though," he added with a grin, "I seem to have lost track of time."

"Oh, dear," she murmured, picturing Powers stepping into the tent and finding them in a passionate embrace. "I'm sorry."

"I'll take my share of the responsibility, but I'm walking you back now."

Outside in the twilight, Rebecca was grateful that Clark set an unhurried pace. She was in no hurry to leave him. Besides, she was sure that their shared passion had left its mark on her face. Her lips felt swollen and her cheeks still burned. She couldn't even guess what might be evident in her eyes.

A change of subject might help, though she had to struggle to think of anything else. "Clark?" she began softly. "When you left me the last couple of nights, you didn't go back to your tent. Where did you go?"

It was a moment before he answered. When he looked down at her she was sure he was having as much trouble as she shaking off the last few minutes. Finally he answered, "I make a round of the camp, check in with each of the guards."

"To make sure they're where they should be?"

He shook his head. "No. I assume each is doing his job. But I know how much a word of encouragement from a superior can mean, especially to raw recruits facing their first threat. Besides, they like to know they're not the only ones losing sleep."

"You always do this?" She hadn't realized that they had stopped walking until he turned to face her.

"That depends on the threat."

"Tonight?"

He looked off in the distance before smiling down at her. "I'd say this is about a four round threat."

"Four?"

He nodded, turning a little more serious. "There are two shifts for guard duty. I try to speak to each guard early in the shift and again toward the end, when it's hardest to stay awake. If I showed up more often than that, they'd believe I was expecting an attack at any moment."

"When do you sleep?"

"When there is no danger." Before she could protest, he added, "I sleep light. And I don't usually lose track of time."

His voice at the end had taken on a sultry timbre that reminded her instantly of what they had just shared. So much for changing the subject.

He took her arm and started her toward the wagon again. When they could make out the figures silhouetted against the canvas sides, he stopped her. She lifted her face toward him, wishing for a good-night kiss, expecting nothing of the kind.

He gently caressed her cheek as he had the night before and she leaned into it. "Good night," he said close to her ear, then turned and left.

"Good night," she whispered, knowing he couldn't hear.

A shouted alarm and a volley of shots brought Rebecca awake with a gasp. She heard Alicia stifle a cry as her Aunt hissed, "What was that?"

"I don't know," she said, throwing off the blanket. She heard the sound of running feet and shouted orders as she quickly threw on the uniform. She tied on her shoes without worrying about socks and rummaged quickly in the bottom of her valise.

"Should I light a lamp?" Alicia whispered.

"No. I found it. Stay here and stay down."

She dropped to the ground with the pistol in her hand as another volley of shots sounded from the north end of camp. She ran toward the sound with a few straggling soldiers.

It was impossible to see more than shapes in the dark, milling soldiers and milling horses. She could only guess what was happening.

"Hold your fire."

She recognized Clark's voice and breathed a sigh of relief. Until that moment she wasn't fully aware of how worried she had been for his safety.

The order was repeated by Sergeant Whiting as a couple more shots cracked in the dark.

"Hold your fire, soldier." She located him as Clark moved to thrust a soldier's rifle barrel toward the ground.

"I coulda got one," the soldier insisted. It was Victor Brooks.

"They're just a small band of young braves out to make names for themselves. They failed to steal our horses. They'll ride back to their elders and never mention this raid. You kill one and we'll have the whole party down on us.

"Sergeant. Send a couple men to check for any casualties."

Brooks wasn't ready to be dismissed. "Weren't we shooting to kill a minute ago?"

Whiting's voice boomed, "Add a 'sir' to that, soldier."

Rebecca heard a grudging, "Sir."

Clark's voice was calm. "That's right, soldier. But we managed to miss them *and* save the horses. I'd like to leave it that way.

"Back to your tents, men."

As the solders dispersed, Rebecca made her way toward Clark. He was talking to the sergeant. "It's less than a hour till dawn. No one's going to get any more sleep. Tell them to light their fires for breakfast, and we'll get under way."

The sergeant left to relay the order, and Clark turned toward Rebecca. "Why am I not surprised to find you here?"

"One of those horses is mine. Besides, if it had been a full-scale attack, you could have used my help." She raised the gun but decided he probably couldn't see it and dropped her arm again.

"If it had been an attack, don't you think I'd have felt better knowing you were safe?" His voice was low and intimate and sent spirals of memory through her body.

"If it had been," she said, just as softly, "there wouldn't have been any place that *was* safe."

He sighed. "That's not something I like to think about."

The admission made her smile. "I'm safe now."

She hadn't realized what emotions he was holding in check until she found herself wrapped in his arms. His chin rested on the top of her head as he held her close. He had been truly worried about her. The realization pleased her.

She reveled in the warmth of his embrace for a moment then drew her head away. She wanted a kiss. She didn't have to ask or tease to get it. His lips came down on hers with a fierce possessiveness so different from his earlier gentle kisses. Liquid fire spread through her body with amazing speed. By the time he ended the kiss, her knees were weak and the pistol felt too heavy for her arm.

"Go back to the ambulance," he whispered.

She wanted to keep his arms around her for a few more minutes. In fact she wasn't sure she could stand without them. "I can't find it in the dark," she said.

He actually chuckled. Well, she hadn't really expected him to believe her.

"You make me forget things," he said, "like time. Responsibilities. Discretion. I should let you stand here until the sun comes up."

He had already turned her toward the wagon, his arm possessively wrapped around her shoulders. She grinned up at him. "Lucky for me you're too much of a gentleman to do that."

She took his grunted response as agreement and swallowed a laugh as she wrapped an arm around his waist.

She wasn't surprised that he didn't allow it. He drew away and tucked her hand into the crook of his arm. This time Rebecca didn't try to hold back the laugh. "It's dark," she reminded him.

"And I'm trying to remain a gentleman."

"Your reputation's safe with me."

"Why am I not reassured?" They had reached the wagon and he turned to face her. "When we march today, I'm going to post extra riders on either side of the ambulance. I want you in it." He touched a finger to her lips when she started to protest. "I need to know that's where you are."

He was being sweetly sincere, but she couldn't resist teasing him. "Is that an order?"

"Ma'am, it would be if I thought it would do any good. How about thinking of it as a favor? And you might want to ask the driver to let you know when the fort's in sight so you can change clothes. I don't think I want to see your father's reaction to your current outfit.''

Rebecca laughed. ''Not to mention the fact that Aunt Belle would be mortified.''

He moved to pull away from her, but she caught his arm. ''Is it over?'' she asked.

''What? The journey? Almost. The danger? I hope so.''

She couldn't put into words what she was really asking so she let him go.

By the time the sun was directly overhead, Rebecca's stomach was complaining. She had eaten very little at breakfast. The anticipated joy at seeing her father again had fought with her disappointment that the journey was nearly over. It would be much more difficult to spend time with Clark unless he chose to call on her.

But surely he would.

Unless he was too intimidated by her father.

Rebecca gave up speculating and gazed off across the prairie. She rode in the wagon. As a favor to Clark, she thought with a smile. She had convinced her aunt that the canvas wouldn't stop an arrow, and they were better off being able to see what was coming. With all four sides rolled up they got the full benefit of the breeze and had a sunshade as well.

Aunt Belle didn't appreciate how comfortable they really were.

"I daresay we should be stopping for lunch soon," Aunt Belle said.

"Maybe not," Rebecca responded, turning toward her companions. "If we're close, it would make more sense to keep traveling."

"Close." The word sounded like a prayer. "I can't imagine ever doing anything but riding in this infernal wagon."

Rebecca cast a longing look toward her gelding that trotted behind. "I could ride up and ask the sergeant how much farther it is."

"You'll do no such thing," Aunt Belle snapped. "We are about to return to civilization and *you* need to remember proper decorum."

Rebecca wasn't daunted by the sharp words. "I simply thought it would be helpful to know. We are planning to dress for civilization, aren't we?"

Aunt Belle seemed to be taking the suggestion seriously. Rebecca held her breath and prayed.

But before Aunt Belle made a decision, Sergeant Whiting rode up to the wagon and turned to trot beside it. "Afternoon, ladies," he said cordially, doffing his hat.

"Why, good afternoon, Mr. Whiting," Rebecca said, knowing her friendly tone would irritate her aunt. "Is everything all right?"

"Yes, ma'am. I figure we'll be getting into Fort

Hays in about an hour and a half. The lieutenant thought you'd like to know.''

"Thank you, Sergeant," Rebecca said. "Please convey our deepest appreciation to the lieutenant and my personal thanks as well. Be sure to mention how much I've enjoyed the ride this morning.''

The sergeant grinned in spite of her scowl.

"An hour and a half!" Aunt Belle repeated, oblivious to the last exchange. "That's barely enough time.

"If you'll excuse us," she said, dismissing the sergeant. "Come girls, help me roll down the sides.''

Knowing they were close enough to the fort to be safe, Rebecca convinced her aunt to let her roll the sides up again once they were dressed. As a result, they got to watch the white smear on the landscape develop into the tent city that was Fort Hays.

Rebecca, her earlier hunger forgotten, found the view stirring.

Aunt Belle was aghast. "This is what passes as civilization in this part of the world? Why, there's nothing here.''

"It's a new fort," Rebecca said. "We'll be here to see it built. Look, there are several buildings under construction. We'll be in a house before winter, I'd imagine.''

"Before winter? Surely there's a town nearby with a hotel.''

There was no use trying to convince her otherwise. Her aunt would find out soon enough how habitable a large army tent could be. Rebecca had always thought they were wonderful as a girl.

The caravan slowed to a walk in order to raise less dust as it followed the road into the collection of tents. Rebecca stood up and searched for her father. When she saw him ahead with a group of other officers she slipped off the back of the wagon and ran to greet him.

She had barely made it past the line of troops and flung her arms around her father when she heard Clark order the troops to halt.

After a brief hug her father disentangled himself and scowled down at her. "Becky girl, I should have known you'd find a way to get here. I can see six years with my sister has had very little effect on you."

Rebecca beamed. "Why thank you, Father."

He chuckled. "I trust she and her daughter have arrived as well, in equally good health."

Rebecca nodded. "They're waiting in the ambulance."

The colonel's attention shifted to something behind her, and she turned to see Clark salute.

"First Lieutenant Clark Forrester reporting, sir."

Rebecca couldn't help but grin. Clark was keeping his eyes carefully off her.

"Welcome, Lieutenant," her father said. "Sergeant, see to the men. The quartermaster will take charge of the supplies. Come inside, Lieutenant, and give me your full report.''

Her father turned toward the tent then stopped, fixing his gaze once again on Rebecca. ''My orderly will show you to our quarters. I'll expect your full report at dinner.''

''Yes, sir.'' She gave him a mock salute.

The colonel entered his tent and Clark moved to follow. As he passed, Rebecca said softly, ''Told you he wouldn't notice my hair.''

He flicked her a glance without the slightest change in his purposeful step.

Colonel Huntington had a two-room tent, or more accurately, two tents with a covered breezeway between. One was used as a bedroom and the other served as kitchen and dining room. The colonel's striker had been sent for, and, after preparing a quick lunch for the ladies, he helped them hang a canvas to separate the bedroom into two and set up three new cots in the larger portion.

''The lack of furniture is deplorable,'' Aunt Belle commented when the last of the trunks had been moved in.

''Your furniture will come with the train,'' Rebecca reminded her. ''Ours is probably stored somewhere.''

Aunt Belle gave her a knowing nod. "Somewhere. But does even your father know where?"

Rebecca laughed. "I'll ask him. Do you want to take a walk around the camp? Get to know your new home?"

Aunt Belle shook her head. "I'm looking forward to lying down on something that doesn't sway. I feel quite worn-out."

"Alicia?"

"I'll go along. If you don't mind, Mother."

"Yes, go. Just stay together and don't speak to anyone."

Rebecca opened her mouth to protest, but decided escape was a better plan. "Have a good rest. We won't be long."

When she and Alicia had walked away from the tent, Rebecca asked, "Have you forgiven me for interfering with you and Brooks?"

Alicia kept her eyes on the ground. "Of course."

"Truly, Alicia, I had your best—"

"Could we not talk about it?"

"All right. What do you want to see first?"

Alicia looked around, considering. "The new buildings. I've been hearing the hammers since we got here."

Rebecca hoped her smile hid her disappointment. She had thought that Alicia might be willing to tell her what had happened the night she had left the wagon. Rebecca didn't need to know everything her cousin did, and she wouldn't care about this if she thought Alicia had put whatever it was behind her. But she didn't. Alicia was too quiet, even for her. She seemed subdued and a little nervous.

Rebecca tried to keep up some carefree banter as they made their way toward the construction site. The tents had been set up a few hundred yards away from the planned fort, and both women were beginning to notice the heat of the day before they arrived.

"I miss the pants already," Rebecca whispered to Alicia as they picked their way between stacks of lumber to find a place to view the work.

Alicia shook her head. "All I miss is the hat."

"I think we should keep the hats," Rebecca said. "We could dress them up with some ribbons and feathers, start a new fashion."

Alicia didn't laugh but at least she smiled.

"Ladies! Ladies!"

Rebecca and Alicia turned to see a stout soldier running toward them. "Good afternoon, Corporal," Rebecca said.

"This is no place for you ladies," the corporal said. "It could be dangerous."

"I can see that," Rebecca said with a smile. "That's why we're clear over here. Tell me, is this to be one of the barracks?"

The corporal turned to watch the workers for a moment. "Why, yes, it is."

"Are you in charge of the project?" Rebecca hoped she sounded suitably impressed.

"In a manner of speaking, ma'am."

"Then, sir, we would so much enjoy a tour of the site."

The corporal turned to smile at them. "Would you, ma'am?"

Rebecca nodded, nudging Alicia so she would do the same.

The corporal seemed to recall himself. "But that's out of the question, ma'am. Too dangerous. Far too dangerous. You best be going back."

Rebecca tried pouting but the corporal was adamant.

"I tried," Rebecca whispered as they made their way slowly back toward the tents.

"You didn't care about a tour," Alicia said. "You just wanted to cause that poor soldier trouble."

"That's unfair, Alicia. Although, I doubt if the man is in charge of anything but seeing that the other men kept working."

"You just don't like to be told what to do."

Rebecca tried to look hurt but gave it up with a shrug. "Let's stop by Father's office on the way back. Maybe he'll give us a tour."

Rebecca was delighted to hear Alicia laugh. "You'd like to see the look on that poor soldier's face if you came back with the post commander."

Rebecca was thinking of a clever quip when she

saw three armed soldiers hurry toward the headquarters tent. One approached the tent entrance as her father stepped out to meet him. Hasty orders were given and the three moved purposefully away.

"What was that about?" Alicia asked.

"I don't know. The soldiers are on guard duty or they wouldn't be armed. Listen, Alicia. I want you to go back to our quarters. I'll go see what's going on. Can you find your way?"

Alicia nodded.

Rebecca hurried forward. She didn't know why she was so worried. Her father could have ordered the arrest of any soldier. For any number of reasons.

But the pure fury she had seen on his face made her wonder if it was somehow personal.

"Father?" she called hesitantly as she entered the tent.

She was surprised to find him alone. And pacing. He turned and scowled at her.

"Father, what's happened?"

He fixed her with a glare she had seen often as a child. It had never bothered her much, but today it made her blood turn cold.

"I've ordered the arrest of Lieutenant Forrester," he said.

Chapter Nine

Rebecca stared at her father for a full minute before she found her voice. "Arrest Clark? Why?"

Her father's eyes narrowed, and she realized she had used the lieutenant's first name. It mattered little under these circumstances. "On what grounds?"

"Dereliction of duty. Endangering his men. Deserting his post. Conduct unbecoming an officer. Anything else I can think of."

What was he talking about? This was not the lieutenant she knew. And loved.

"On whose word?" she asked, hoping with enough information she could understand what had happened. And correct it.

The colonel sighed and slumped in his chair. It creaked under his weight. The oak chair and its matching desk seemed out of place in a tent.

Rebecca shook her head. The whole conversation was out of place.

"A soldier," her father began, "reported seeing the lieutenant with a young woman in his arms last night in the midst of a hostile attack."

Rebecca opened her mouth but he waved for silence. "He said he couldn't tell which of the young ladies was with the lieutenant but it isn't hard for me to guess."

Rebecca took a step forward. "You believed him?"

"Of course I did," her father shouted, coming to his feet. "I know my daughter! Your aunt has kept me well posted on your activities."

Rebecca's heart was pounding in her ears. Somehow she had to make him see reason. All of Clark's comments about the trouble she could cause him came back to her. "The attack was over," she said.

The colonel nodded slowly. "So it's true, isn't it? The attack was over…by the time you went to him? If this soldier saw you in his arms, what else happened that he didn't see?"

Rebecca felt her cheeks warm. "You can't do this to him," she whispered. She had brought this on Clark. There had to be a way to save him.

Her father watched her, a speculative gleam in his eyes. "Why not?"

Rebecca swallowed. "Because…we're planning to be married. If you court-martial him, it'll ruin my life as well."

He stepped toward her. "Is that the truth?"

Rebecca nodded. "I love him, Father."

"I suppose that changes things," he said, moving back to his chair. "It puts me in a damnable position, though. The man takes liberties with my daughter using promises of marriage to break down her resistance."

Rebecca rolled her eyes. "Father."

The colonel ignored her. "Is there any reason the wedding can't take place this evening?"

"This evening?"

"Yes, of course. The fort being in the condition it is, there's little use trying to plan some huge celebration anyway. Might as well get the deed done, don't you think?"

He was watching her closely. He was expecting a protest! Well, he wouldn't get one from her. Clark was another matter. "I need to talk to him."

"Out of the question. You go home and do what you can to make the tent presentable. I'll talk to your lieutenant."

"But Father—" But what? She couldn't hardly tell him she needed to explain the situation to Clark. How furious would her father be when he found out there had been no such promises exchanged? Surely he would force the marriage rather than go ahead with the court-martial!

"Come, girl. I'll see you make it home without

getting lost. We can explain the situation to Belle together.''

Rebecca stifled a groan.

One empty little tent, separated from the rest, was designated as the guardhouse. Clark stretched out on the ground and tried to be grateful that he hadn't simply been chained to a tree. Not that having his ankles and wrists in shackles was much more comfortable. He was at least out of public view.

He had known from the beginning that any involvement with the colonel's daughter would mean trouble, though he hadn't anticipated quite this much. And exactly why he was in chains was still a mystery.

He seriously doubted if his current predicament was caused by anything Rebecca had said. Of course, confronted with her behavior she would probably weep and say whatever was necessary to protect herself.

He frowned at the image. He had been thoroughly convinced of that a week ago. He wasn't so certain now.

He unbuttoned his blouse and removed the bundle from the inside pocket. Rebecca's hair wrapped tightly in a handkerchief. He didn't open it; the danger of being interrupted was too great. It was enough to hold it in his hands and let it stimulate memories of Rebecca.

It smelled faintly of smoke. It had been with him when he had sifted through the ashes with her. The only time it had been out of the pocket was when his uniform had been washed.

At first he had regretted that the smoke had contaminated his treasure, but now it reminded him that Rebecca wasn't quite the frivolous girl she had once seemed.

He closed his eyes. He had let himself hope that with her father's consent he could call upon her, court her. In his fantasies he even won her. Obviously her father was going to be harder to convince than he had thought.

He heard voices outside the tent, someone speaking to the guard. He tucked the bundle away and rolled to his feet. The last button was back in place as Colonel Huntington ducked into the tent.

The colonel stood for a moment then spoke over his shoulder. "Bring a light. I want to see the prisoner's face."

Clark shifted position as he waited. The clank of the chains made him wish he had held still. They sounded somehow hopeless. Not exactly what he wanted to portray during this interview.

The guard finally brought a lantern and set it on the ground.

"Are the chains necessary?" Huntington asked.

"There are no bars, sir."

The colonel took a step closer to Clark. "Do I have your word you won't try to escape?"

Clark couldn't conceal his surprise. "Yes, sir."

"Remove the shackles."

The guard complied quickly but left the chains lying on the ground, a silent reminder that they would be restored as soon as the colonel left.

"Thank you, sir," Clark said, rubbing a numbed wrist.

"Do you know the charges against you?"

Clark took two slow breaths. "No, sir."

"There are a number of formal charges I can make but basically it comes down to seducing my daughter."

Clark kept his eyes locked with the colonel's. "There may be some truth in that, sir."

"Did you leave your post during a battle for a tryst with Rebecca?"

Clark blinked. "No, sir."

Huntington waved a hand in the air as if he had somehow become sidetracked. He paced for a moment, studying the ground. He stopped directly in front of Clark. "Do you love Rebecca?"

Clark wished he knew what Rebecca had said to her father, and he to her. The question could be a trap, perhaps more for Rebecca than for himself.

"Sir," he began, choosing his words carefully. "I tried to see that your daughter and I were never alone. I meant to protect her reputation. But it is true that I encouraged her visits. And I'll accept the blame for whatever damage was done."

"Hmm." The colonel nodded. "Interesting. But it

doesn't answer my question. Are you in love with my daughter?''

With no understanding of where this was leading, Clark decided on honesty. "Yes, sir."

Huntington spent another moment pacing. Whether it was to help him formulate his next question or to increase his prisoner's concern, Clark couldn't guess. Though it was definitely doing the latter.

Abruptly the colonel stopped. "I understand there were certain promises made."

"Sir?"

"Namely marriage."

Clark swallowed. What was going on? "Is that what she said?"

"Are you denying it?"

Clark hesitated. "No, sir."

Huntington seemed to find that amusing. Clark was too bewildered to guess why.

He slapped Clark on the back. "The girl pleaded for your career, Lieutenant. It seems if you're court-martialed it'll ruin her life as well, since she's determined to keep her promise under any circumstances and marry you."

"I see," Clark said, and thought he did. She was trying to take responsibility for her actions as she had when her flirting lessons had gotten Alicia into trouble. It was a noble sacrifice, one he couldn't accept. "May I talk to your daughter, sir?"

The colonel shook his head. "Nope. She's getting

ready for the wedding. You should do the same. You can see her at my quarters in say…an hour.''

"Sir, I'd like to talk to her first.''

Huntington looked significantly down at the shackles and back at Clark. "In an hour. In your dress uniform. Prepared to make her your wife.''

Clark walked toward Colonel Huntington's quarters certain that no bridegroom had ever had quite the same case of jitters. But few bridegrooms were ordered to their wedding by their commanding officer.

There was still a possibility that there would be no wedding. He would arrive at the Huntington tent several minutes before the appointed time. Surely the colonel wouldn't deny him the opportunity to speak to Rebecca alone. He had to know why she had lied to her father. Unless this marriage was what she truly wanted, he wouldn't go through with it.

The idea brought a sinking feeling to the pit of his stomach. Returning to the jail tent wasn't nearly as demoralizing as learning that Rebecca had no true feeling for him. For a moment he wished he could simply not ask.

In the breezeway between the two tents, Clark softly called her name. The openings to the tents faced each other. He could hear muffled women's voices behind the closed flap of one.

"Forrester!'' came a hearty voice from the other. Huntington clapped him on the back and all but pulled him into the tent. "You're early. That shows more eagerness than I expected."

The sparsely furnished room was bedecked with wildflowers, no small feat on such short notice. Still it was hardly the wedding she had no doubt dreamed of.

"I need to talk to Rebecca, sir."

"She's still getting dressed," the colonel said, moving to a small cupboard and collecting a bottle and two glasses. "Can I get you a drink?"

"No, thank you. Sir, I need to know this is what she wants."

The colonel poured a splash of whiskey into each of the glasses and brought them toward Clark. "Have a drink and stop worrying about it."

"Sir, I have no intention of marrying your daughter against her will."

"It was her idea, wasn't it?" Huntington smiled and urged the glass into Clark's hand. He raised his own. "To marriage."

Clark refused to return the toast. "I have nothing against marriage and certainly nothing against the idea of marriage to your daughter. But if she's doing this because of some sense of responsibility for my career..."

"Forrester, you've known Rebecca for what? Eight, ten days? You know she's a manipulative little flirt."

Clark took a sip of the whiskey.

"I'll be glad to see her safely married," the colonel continued. "To be honest, son, I'd feel a little sorry for you, except I figure a man used to commanding troops ought to be able to keep her in line."

Clark couldn't resist. "You haven't, sir."

Huntington chuckled. "She's my daughter. It's different. Wait until you have one of your own."

Huntington set his empty glass on the table then changed his mind and hid it beside the bottle in the cupboard.

"That brings up another subject," he said returning to stand in front of Clark. "I recommend that you get the girl pregnant right away. A child to look after should settle her down."

Clark was sure the shock he felt must show on his face. "If you don't mind my saying so, sir, your daughter comes by her talent for manipulation quite honestly."

Huntington laughed. "You said you love her. I'm doing you a favor."

"Sirs?"

They both turned toward the open tent flap.

"What is it, Sergeant?" the colonel asked.

Clark stepped forward. "I asked Sergeant Whiting to serve as my witness, sir."

"Well, come in and toast the bridegroom," the colonel said, returning to the cupboard.

"My pleasure, sir." The sergeant leaned close to Clark. "You should hear the rumors, sir."

Clark motioned him to silence. Rumors were the least of his concerns right now. And without a chance to talk to Rebecca, he saw no choice but to go through with this marriage made by Colonel Huntington.

Or maybe he didn't want a choice. He could tell the colonel right now that he was returning to the guardhouse. That he wasn't letting Rebecca sacrifice her freedom.

Instead, he watched Huntington hand a glass to Whiting and raise his refilled glass. "To the bride-groom."

Clark downed the last of his whiskey.

The chaplain arrived and Huntington poured another round of drinks. Clark took only a sip and deposited the glass in the cupboard with the rest when the colonel went to tell the ladies that he would abide no more waiting.

"That's enough, Aunt Belle. There's nothing more you can do for my hair."

Rebecca had sat through what seemed like hours of lecturing, though it couldn't possibly have been that long. The upshot of it all was that Aunt Belle felt extremely sorry for poor Lieutenant Forrester. He was getting a frivolous, selfish wife who would likely continue to flirt with other men. A cruel trick since he was marrying her to save her reputation. Rebecca's only chance of avoiding marital disaster was to become a serious, hardworking wife, a miracle Aunt Belle did not imagine she would live to see.

Earlier, while Alicia was out picking flowers, Aunt Belle had shared her knowledge of men and their needs as well as a wife's responsibilities. The information implied that the stolen kisses were most likely the last of the fun. Belle's assertion that a man might enjoy a flirtation with a stranger but would be disgusted by the same behavior in a wife seemed entirely unfair.

Rebecca knew Aunt Belle had heard her father's summons, but still the woman fussed with a curl that failed to hide one of the many pins that held flowers in her hair. "It looks fine, Aunt Belle."

"I guess it's the best we can do," Belle said with a sigh. "Alicia, are you ready?"

"Yes, Mother."

Rebecca stood and turned to her cousin who sat on a cot in the far corner of the tent. Alicia seemed more in horror of Rebecca's sudden marriage than her mother did. Aunt Belle was of course pleased to be rid of her.

"Then I suppose we should proceed," Aunt Belle said, "before your father yells at us again. I'll go first and send your father back to escort you. Alicia, you go in just ahead of them."

Rebecca laughed. "It seems a little odd to stick to tradition at this point."

Aunt Belle's answer was an unladylike grunt.

"Alicia," Rebecca said, taking advantage of a moment alone. "Don't worry about me. I'm marrying the man I love."

"I thought you didn't believe in love."

"I didn't. But I do now. Please don't be so frightened."

Alicia took a step toward her, looking more anguished than ever. "If I'm caught kissing a man, will he make me marry him?"

Rebecca wished she could assure her cousin that it wouldn't happen, but she wasn't so sure. "He's not making me marry Clark...exactly. This was my idea."

"So he's making Clark marry you. Somehow that's worse."

Rebecca didn't know how to answer her cousin. Her father didn't give her a chance, anyway. He stepped into the tent and took her arm. She had to hold him back long enough to give Alicia a head start.

She stepped out of one tent and into another and saw Clark waiting for her. Her heart seemed to skip a beat. He was so handsome. And so serious. She wanted to see that eyebrow quirk up in surprise. A dimpled smile would probably do it, but she was too nervous to manage it.

Her father put her hand in Clark's and they turned to face the chaplain. The ceremony was brief. To

Rebecca's surprise, it was her father who produced the ring.

"It was Rebecca's mother's," he said, handing it to Clark. "Since I have no son to pass it to, I want her to have it."

"Thank you, sir," Clark said, then slipped the ring on Rebecca's finger.

"I pronounce you man and wife," the chaplain said. "You may kiss the bride."

Clark's kiss was brief and entirely too chaste. He was as nervous as she. Or perhaps she wasn't nervous at all. Perhaps what she felt was anticipation. Clark's earlier kisses had made her long for something more, something only partially understood.

But Aunt Belle's words confused her. She wanted to be a good wife to Clark. Aunt Belle might know better than she what that meant. Perhaps, she decided, she would take her cue from Clark.

Colonel Huntington poured another round and toasted the new couple. Then Clark, with Rebecca's hand firmly clutching his, led the way out of the tent. The other officers were waiting and sent up a cheer at their appearance. A command performance, Rebecca assumed, since few of them knew Clark.

They started toward Clark's tent with the crowd following.

Clark leaned close to Rebecca's ear. "When I moved into my tent, I didn't know I'd be sharing it."

Rebecca hadn't thought of that. Of course Clark's

tent wouldn't be as large as her father's. "We'll be a little crowded but it's only for a few months."

"Space wasn't exactly my concern."

"What then?"

His voice dropped even lower. "Rebecca, I can't provide you with even the most basic of comforts."

Rebecca pictured herself wrapped comfortably in his arms and smiled. "What," she murmured, "do you consider basic comforts?"

"A bed. A stove. A floor."

Rebecca had to laugh. "Until the fort's built, we all live like this."

They had reached the tent, and Clark and Rebecca turned to face the crowd. Rebecca counted only two women besides her relatives. The other wives, she guessed, were waiting for the quarters to be built before joining their husbands.

"I thank you, gentlemen and ladies," Clark said in his smooth drawl, "for your good wishes. If you would excuse us now, my wife and I...have some things to discuss."

Rebecca's cheeks grew warm from the laughter that followed his remark. She turned toward the tent. Clark reached around her to raise the flap. She stepped inside and felt him enter behind her. The sight that greeted them made her laugh. "Someone's taken care of your first concern, anyway."

It was definitely the ugliest bed she had ever seen. It looked like the frame had been made of scrap lumber. The mattress was three mismatched ticks split open and stitched together. It seemed a little long for its width, or perhaps a little narrow for its length. And it took up at least a third of the entire tent.

"Sergeant Whiting!"

Clark had left the tent, and Rebecca hurried after him. Most of the crowd had started to disperse, but several officers turned back at the lieutenant's shout.

"Yes, sir, Lieutenant?" Whiting saluted then removed his hat. "Afternoon again, Mrs. Forrester."

"Afternoon, Mr. Whiting," Rebecca said, grinning at the mischievous twinkle in the older man's eyes.

"I assume you know something about this," Clark said, with the slightest tip of his head toward the tent.

"The tent, sir?"

"The bed, Sergeant."

"Ah. Yes, sir. I put four of my best men on it. The mattress is stuffed with fresh straw, but that's about the only thing I'm vouching for." He leaned toward Clark. "So you might want to take it easy on it, sir."

Clark was silent for a long moment. Rebecca knew she should be embarrassed. They were after all joking about what would surely happen on that monstrous bed that night. And she *was* a little embarrassed. But she was also fighting down a giggle. Nerves, perhaps.

Clark cleared his throat. "Well, Sergeant. Thank them for me." With a final nod, he turned and motioned Rebecca back inside, following close behind.

While Clark lit a lamp, Rebecca eyed her wedding present. "Is it safe?" she asked, hearing the giggle in her voice.

Clark stepped cautiously toward the bed, and she bit back another laugh. Clark grabbed one of the rough boards on the frame and shook it. To Rebecca's surprise the bed barely trembled. He lifted the mattress. "At least they used new rope," he said.

"It's beautiful, Clark," Rebecca said. "I'm sure we'll cherish it for years to come."

His eyebrow shot up, and she gave in to the laughter. He laughed too, easing some of the tension. If he had given her the slightest sign, she would have walked into his arms. But he didn't, and, while she wanted to touch him, she wanted more than anything else to follow his wishes.

Rebecca lay as still as possible, staring into the darkness. She didn't know if Clark slept. He was still. Silent. He was near enough that she could sense his presence but at the same time he was completely out of reach.

She had watched him all evening for any sign that he would welcome her touch, that he longed for a kiss as much as she did. But she saw none.

He helped her arrange the tent when her trunks arrived. He hung a canvas beside the bed, dividing the tent into two rooms. He was pleasant. Respectful. Quiet.

Wasn't that always his manner? She looked back on the short time that she had known him. He had kept his feelings carefully hidden. Even when she flirted outrageously he had done little more than quirk a brow.

But he had kissed her! More than once. She had assumed he had liked it as much as she did. Now she wondered if he had kissed her only because he knew that was what she wanted. Had he been the polite, accommodating gentleman?

Well, he could be a gentleman again! She wanted to be kissed, and she would just tell him so.

No she wouldn't, she realized. He had married her to save his career, a career her own thoughtlessness had come close to destroying. And, as her aunt had said, he may have made the sacrifice to protect her reputation. She wouldn't add to his misery by forcing herself on him.

She felt tears sting her eyes and closed them tight, hoping to stem the flow. He would never know how unhappy she was. She would make his home as comfortable as possible. She would try to do just what he wanted. Maybe, if she was a perfect wife, he would grow to love her as much as she loved him.

Clark rolled cautiously out of bed. There was little room between the bed and the side of the tent and he eased along until he could slip around the divider and enter the other room. He had slept, but not very much. There was probably an hour until dawn, but he knew his rest was over.

His body ached for her. Her warmth had heated his blood. The sheet that covered him had come from her trunk and carried the same dried-flower scent that clung to her clothes. He had been conscious of even the slightest movement, the tiniest sigh while she slept. He had never felt such desire.

Where had the little flirt gone? He could have silenced the tease with his kisses. One suggestive grin would have sent him tumbling into that ridiculous bed with Rebecca in his arms.

But she wasn't flirting now. She didn't want him. She had married him out of some misguided desire to atone for her earlier behavior, behavior for which he was equally to blame.

And he shouldn't have let her. He should have spent the night on the ground with shackles on his hands and feet. God knew, he would probably have slept better.

He had listened to his heart and ignored everything else. It was too late to go back now. He had tied her to him, and he would do his best to make her happy.

The thought nearly filled him with panic. He had no idea how to do that. What did she want? What did she expect? He thought back on everything she had said. She loved the prairie. She loved riding. He smiled to himself. Having donkeys for pets she had said. Maybe it wouldn't be impossible after all.

But she also loved to flirt. It was part of her nature.

It took him a moment to sort out the implications of that thought. If she had no interest in flirting with him, would she flirt with other men? If he objected, would she turn into a stern, bitter woman like her aunt?

He shook his head and ran his hand through his hair. It wasn't worth thinking about. They had only had one evening together. She had no doubt been nervous. Her dimpled smile would be back, her sparkling eyes. She would tease him and he wouldn't have to resist.

He left the tent to light a fire. He would warm some water and shave. Start coffee for their breakfast. As he went about the tasks his thoughts kept returning to his wife. What if he was wrong? What if she didn't want him? What would he do the first time she turned those eyes on someone else?

He stared into the tiny fire as if he would find the answer there. After a moment he sighed. God help him, it would break his heart, but he would allow her that freedom.

Chapter Ten

Rebecca woke to the smell of coffee. Realization of where she was came to her instantly. She sprang out of bed and wrapped a light robe around herself as she slipped past the canvas curtain. Sleeping late didn't quite fit with her plans to be a perfect wife.

The room was lit by a single lamp. In the soft glow she made out the camp desk, already set for breakfast. She approached it and stared down at delicate china dishes. She lifted a bowl and tipped it toward the light. The soft pink roses looked like painted needlepoint.

"They were my mother's."

She looked up to find Clark just inside the tent. He carried a small pot to the table and emptied its contents into the two bowls. "Oatmeal," he said. "Not a particularly elegant breakfast but something I can manage."

"You didn't need to do this."

"I wanted to." He stood watching her for a moment then seemed to catch himself. "I'll bring the coffee."

As he left the tent, Rebecca sighed. He was off to a better start as a wife than she was.

When he returned with the coffee she noticed his eyes flick over her before he filled the cups.

"I should get dressed," she said.

His response came quickly. "No. Eat it while it's hot. That was the idea, you know. To let you sleep."

"Thank you," she said, slipping into one of the folding chairs.

"I'm sorry we don't have any cream, but there is sugar," he said as he sat across from her.

"They say this is very good for you." She wondered if she should reach for the sugar or wait until he had taken some. She thought her uncle had always served himself first, but she hadn't ever paid that much attention.

"At least if you're a horse."

"What?" Her mind had wondered. "Oh. The oats." She smiled and reached for the sugar bowl. Eating would give her something to do besides feel foolish.

"Speaking of horses," Clark said, taking the sugar when she passed it to him and sprinkling a liberal portion over his cereal. "You should ride yours today."

It seemed like a frivolous pastime, but an attractive

one. "I'm not sure I'll have time," she said, hoping no hint of disappointment rang in her voice.

"You should take the time," he said. "He'll turn wild on you if you don't."

Of course. The horse was valuable, one of her few assets, and she should protect it.

"You can wear the pants if you want."

She looked up, surprised. "Wouldn't that be scandalous?"

He was watching her face, trying to find something. She didn't know what. She averted her eyes and tasted the oatmeal.

"Rebecca," he said. "I'm sure everyone here has heard how you dressed on the journey. And after yesterday, what could it possibly hurt?"

Rebecca understood. He wasn't serious, of course. He was reminding her how much damage she had already done. She ate quickly, hoping he wouldn't speak to her again, afraid if he did she couldn't meet his eyes.

The notes of reveille sounded, followed immediately by stable call. Of course there were no stables yet. The horses had been turned into a corral, Rebecca's gelding with them. Each cavalryman had the responsibility for the care of his own mount. Officers might care for their own or leave it to their striker. She didn't know which her husband did. She did know she wasn't going out to the corral at the same moment as the entire cavalry.

"I need to go," Clark said, rising.

Rebecca looked up, barely meeting his eyes before she lowered her head again.

"I don't know where I'll be at noon. Why don't you eat lunch with your family?"

She nodded, forcing a smile. "I'll see you tonight, then."

He lingered for a moment. When he moved, instead of leaving immediately, he bent and kissed the top of her head. "Have a pleasant day," he whispered.

That kiss was the first touch since the wedding. She wanted to take it as an invitation and throw herself into his arms, but he was already moving away.

Alone, Rebecca considered what she should do. She needed to make some kind of arrangement for the gelding. She didn't want to hire anyone. What money she had should be saved to furnish their house once it was built.

On top of that, she had to figure out how to run a household. Or rather a tent. Her aunt wouldn't be much help there. She should talk to the women she had seen with the officers.

Shortly after the trumpet call for the sick marcher to take sick soldiers to the post hospital, Rebecca left the tent. She had washed the dishes and packed them carefully back in the crate, tidied the tent as much as possible, and dressed in her most practical skirt and blouse. Everyone else would have finished with his horse and reported for duty. She should be alone at the corral.

But she wasn't. As she approached, she saw a soldier dressed in a white stable frock about to exit the corral. When he turned to face her, she recognized Mr. Powers.

"Morning, Miss...Mrs. Forrester."

She smiled. "Good morning. Did you sleep late?"

"No, ma'am. I took the liberty of caring for your horse." He blushed a little at the admission. "I hope you don't mind."

"Not at all. Thank you. I was just coming to do that."

He nodded and was about to move on when she noticed the collar of the cotton frock had come loose and been resewn in a very haphazard manner. "Mr. Powers," she said quickly. "Would you be willing to continue with that task?"

"Yes, ma'am." He seemed honored by the request.

She had no intention of imposing, however. "I can't pay you, but I could do your mending for you."

Powers touched his collar. "That seems more than fair, ma'am."

She smiled. "If you find the time, could you ride him once in a while?"

He nodded and hurried away. She knew fatigue call would sound in a few minutes and he needed to be ready to report. She hoped the care of a second horse wouldn't cause him trouble. She would have to remember to ask when he brought his mending.

She wrinkled her nose at the prospect. She wasn't fond of sewing. But she could, and was at least better at it than he was. If he needed anything too complicated like an alteration, she would have to call on Alicia for help. And do her a favor in exchange.

With a sigh, she headed back toward the officers' tents. She would call on Aunt Belle and Alicia first. Perhaps they had already met the other wives and could introduce her.

Aunt Belle set aside her sewing and greeted Rebecca rather suspiciously, as if she expected to learn Rebecca had already been thrown out by her husband. Alicia glanced up from a book, returned Rebecca's smile, and went back to her reading.

"I'm on my way to meet the other wives," Rebecca said. "Have you met them yet?"

"Only briefly. But you're right, it is our responsibility to call on them. Come along, Alicia."

Alicia opened her mouth to protest then closed it and her book at the same time. "Yes, Mother," she murmured.

Belle led the way. "We will visit Captain Morton's wife first. Her name is Jennifer. She is quite acceptable for you to befriend, I believe."

The comment was directed at Rebecca and did not

seem to include Alicia. A married woman would not make a suitable friend for the girl, Rebecca supposed.

Belle stopped outside a tent very near her own and called in an overly-pleasant voice, "Yoo-hoo. Mrs. Morton. Are you in?"

A pretty dark-haired woman pulled aside the flap. "Where else would I be? There's absolutely nothing to do here."

"Exactly," Belle agreed.

"Come in, Mrs. Evans. Miss Evans." Her eyes narrowed as Rebecca passed. "And I finally get to meet the new Mrs. Forrester. You snagged quite a looker, if you don't mind my saying so."

"Not at all," Rebecca said. "I haven't seen your husband so I'm not prepared to assess what *you* snagged."

"Rebecca! You'll have to excuse my niece," Belle said. "She is too outspoken for her own good."

Mrs. Morton laughed airily and waved one hand in the air as if brushing aside an apology.

Rebecca was surprised to discover the floor of Mrs. Morton's tent was covered with Persian rugs, some already damaged by mud. The chairs, both of them, belonged in a parlor and took up far too much room in the crowded tent. Mrs. Morton sat down in one of these and said, "I'd offer you ladies tea, but my striker's gone and I'm afraid I can't boil water."

They all laughed with her, but Rebecca suspected

the woman wasn't exaggerating. So much for learning anything from her.

Belle took the remaining seat, and Alicia and Rebecca sat together on a trunk. Rebecca held her tongue while her aunt and Mrs. Morton traded miseries. Feeling the press of time, Rebecca finally came to her feet.

"Please excuse me," she said, "but I hoped to call on the other woman yet this morning."

"Mrs. Raymond? I daresay you won't find her very pleasant." Mrs. Morton cast her other companions a knowing smile.

"Rebecca," Aunt Belle said, "what are you thinking? It's hours until noon."

Rebecca tried not to show her impatience. "Of course you're right. And since none of you will be preparing the noon meal you should certainly stay and visit. Would you direct me to Mrs. Raymond's tent?"

Mrs. Morton gave her the directions, and Rebecca bade them goodbye. She would have liked to rescue Alicia but knew Aunt Belle would object. She left the tent without a twinge of guilt over the false impression she had given them. She wouldn't be preparing a noon meal either, except for herself.

The Raymond tent wasn't exactly where Mrs. Morton had said it would be. In fact nothing was. But, as Rebecca was looking around for someone else to ask, Mrs. Raymond stepped out of a double tent and poured the contents of a dishpan into a series of potted plants.

"Mrs. Raymond?" Rebecca asked as she approached.

"Yes?" The woman turned and smiled in recognition. She was probably close to forty, very trim and neat. "You're the new bride," she said, reaching a hand out to Rebecca.

"Yes," Rebecca said, taking the damp hand. "I'm out meeting the other ladies this morning."

"I'm Opal. Come inside," she said, leading the way. "You can't imagine how thrilled I was to discover there were going to be three more women here. You've met Jennifer?"

"My aunt and cousin are visiting with Mrs. Morton now."

Opal laughed. "Call her Jennifer. It'll annoy her."

The inside of Opal's tent was at once practical and homey. There was no unnecessary clutter but a small jar of flowers graced the table and a family portrait hung on one canvas wall.

Opal quickly filled a kettle with water and, excusing herself, left the tent. In a moment she was back. "The stove heats up the tent too much so we put it outside," she explained. "We'll have tea in a minute and you can tell me all about yourself and that handsome husband of yours."

Rebecca shook her head. "I'd rather you tell me how to run a household."

"Without a house," Opal added for her.

"Exactly."

Two hours later, Rebecca's head was full of half-formed ideas. She now knew where to find eggs and milk, she just didn't now what she would trade for them. But her first task would be bartering fresh game from Opal's son.

The boy came in right when Opal said they could expect him. He was tall, with the muscled body of a young man but the face of a fifteen-year-old. He grinned shyly when his mother introduced him to Rebecca.

"Your mother's been bragging about your hunting skills, Hank," Rebecca said.

"I'm pretty good," he replied modestly.

"I understand you sell what your family can't eat. I was wondering if there was anything I might do for you in exchange for some mcat." Saying it aloud suddenly made it sound foolish. Surely this boy's efficient mother could provide anything he might want.

Still the boy looked thoughtful. He glanced at his mother, shuffled his feet and cleared his throat. "Might you know how to dance, Mrs. Forrester?"

"Dance?"

"Yes, ma'am," the boy replied in a rush. "When the rest of the families get here there'll be dances. I know a couple of the officers have daughters and there might be some settlers with girls, too. I don't want to step on their toes or nothin' but I don't want to stand in the back and watch like when I was a kid, neither.''

"Dancing lessons," Rebecca said, nodding. "I think I can do that." She tried to picture the tall boy leading her around a dance floor. Then she tried to imagine Clark's reaction. Maybe this wasn't a good idea.

But the boy was already beaming. "Gee, thanks, ma'am. I'll try to bag ya something every day. I shot lots of quail this morning. You could have two or even three, maybe, after Ma picks what she wants." He shuffled his feet again, pointed behind himself, added, "I'll go dress 'em," and left the tent.

Rebecca turned to find Opal grinning at her. "*I* could teach the boy to dance. Do you think he's ever mentioned this to me? Not on your life."

Rebecca laughed. "I'm glad. I was afraid I was going to be taking on more sewing."

With Opal's instructions for roasting quail tucked in her bodice, Rebecca set out to find Private Malone. Opal said he had four chickens in a cage behind his tent. He claimed to have bought them from a passing settler, though Opal was dubious. Whatever their origin, he took good care of them and sold the eggs at a dear price.

Recall from fatigue had already sounded, and she knew the men would have approximately two hours before they were called back to duty. In a normal fort, she would never have dreamed of invading their mess hall, but camp rules still applied and Malone would be assigned with three messmates to share meal responsibilities however they chose.

Opal's directions were better than Jennifer's, but even if they hadn't been the gentle clucking of the hens would have led her to Malone's tent once she got close.

She approached a group of soldiers intent on building a fire. "Is Private Malone here?"

"Aye, lass." One of the men stood. Evidence of several fights decorated a hard face. "Be ye an angel come to save this poor sinner?"

His companions laughed.

Rebecca smiled. "I came to barter for some eggs and if preaching's your price, I'd be happy to oblige."

"She's a shrewd one, Paddy," one of the soldiers said. "You best watch yourself."

Paddy didn't look near as tough when he was smiling. "Let's be discussing this in private, miss," he said, stepping away from the others. "It is miss, isn't it?"

"Mrs. Forrester," she said, not making a move to follow him.

His companions murmured their concern for the life of poor Paddy after joking with an officer's wife.

Paddy turned toward Rebecca and gave a gallant little bow. "I prefer to do me negotiatin' in private, if you would be so kind as to step out o' the hearin' of these rascals. They be jealous o' me hens, truth be known.''

After a moment of hesitation, Rebecca followed the private around the side of his tent. She was barely out of the other soldiers' sight and not out of earshot if she raised her voice. Still the situation made her nervous.

''Ye said barter, ma'am,'' Paddy began in a low voice. ''I reckon ye be sayin' there's no money for Paddy. What service might ye want to offer me?''

It came to Rebecca suddenly exactly what service the man could be thinking of. It hadn't even crossed her mind that this could be dangerous. ''Sewing, perhaps,'' she said quickly.

''I can stitch a seam as fine as any woman,'' he whispered. ''I've somethin' else in mind.''

''Mr. Malone,'' she began, but he cut her off with a wave and a grin.

''Can ye read, ma'am? And write?''

''Of course. Do you want me to teach you?'' She wasn't sure she was up to the task, but if that was what this man wanted, she'd do her best, with or without the eggs. Everyone should be able to read.

He shook his head and laughed. ''I be way too old, ma'am. But there's folks back home what I'd like to be writin' to. Could you do it for me?''

Rebecca nodded slowly.

"See, me friends there, they don't know I canna read. You'll keep me secret?"

"Of course," she whispered.

"I got no eggs today," he said, "but I'll bring 'em by in a day or two."

He held out a hand to close the deal and Rebecca shook it. With a nod she turned to leave. Behind her one of the other soldiers asked, "Did you get a deal, Paddy?"

"Come Sunday, the angel's gonna save me soul."

"I'm a sinner, too, ma'am," the other soldier called.

Rebecca was thoughtful as she walked back to her tent. So far she had promised to do one man's mending, write letters for another and teach a boy to dance. That didn't seem like too much to do, especially considering that housecleaning only took ten minutes. No, it was all going very well, as long as she didn't run out of skills to barter.

The tent seemed lonely when she entered it, not at all like a home. She sat down on one of the chairs and looked around critically. What was missing?

Memories, she decided. If it looked like Clark's tent on the march, with his cot at one side, and the folding desk with the chess set in the center, it wouldn't seem lonely. She smiled to herself. They needed to make some new memories.

She felt her smile fade as worries invaded her

mind. She brushed them away. Tonight's dinner might make the difference.

And in the meantime, there were lots of things to do. She needed to go to the quartermaster, find out if Clark had collected all the food issued to him, and determine the size of his current debt at the commissary.

She wrinkled her nose. Running a tab at the commissary was really something she should discuss with Clark. She was reluctant to do so because she wanted to manage everything herself. How would she prove she was a perfect wife if she had to ask his permission to purchase every little thing?

With a sigh, she stood and walked to the crate that stored the foodstuffs. She would think of something. Though what, she couldn't imagine. The quartermaster could read, or he wouldn't have that job. He no doubt knew how to dance as well and probably had some arrangement for mending. At least in the case of the last, she hoped so. She truly hated to sew.

Clark caught the smell of roasting fowl as he made his way toward his tent. The scent wasn't especially surprising on the prairie, but finding his wife tending the birds over an open fire was.

He paused to study her profile. She was crouched near the fire, her skirts tucked carefully beneath her knees. Little wisps of dark hair danced in the heat.

A bead of sweat trickled down her flushed cheek, and she brushed it away with a rolled-up sleeve.

She lifted a pan from the edge of the fire with only a folded towel to protect her fingers, and held it beneath a bird. With a small paintbrush she basted it, catching the excess back in the pan.

Fear that she would burn herself propelled him forward. He had his gloves on before he reached her. He knelt, closer to her than was necessary, and took the pan from her.

"You startled me," she said, drawing a little away from the fire, bringing her shoulder up against his.

"I didn't want to do that," he said. His free arm went around her, steadying her unnecessarily. Her face was turned up toward his and for a moment he forgot about their dinner sizzling in front of them. What would those flushed lips taste like?

"Do you think they look good?" she asked just above a whisper.

Clark blinked then pulled his eyes away from her face. She was speaking of the birds, of course. "They look wonderful. Let me help you finish."

He held the pan while she basted each bird. "This is quite a surprise," he said as they worked. "Don't tell me you can hunt, too?"

She smiled. "As a matter of fact, I can. Or at least I used to. But I got these from Hank, Major Raymond's son."

He didn't want to know how she talked the boy

out of them. A dimpled smile would probably do it. Just how old was the major's son, anyway?

Clark helped Rebecca remove the meat from the spit and carried the platter into the tent. She went ahead of him with a bowl of rice she had kept warm near the fire. The table was set with a jar of wildflowers in the center.

"It's impossible to find any fresh vegetables," she said, "except onions. There are some canned goods at the commissary."

"Buy what you want. They'll keep a tab of it."

"Is that all right?"

He had stepped up beside her to set the platter down. He didn't want to move away to take his seat. She didn't seem in any hurry either. He wished she would give him some sign that she wanted his touch. "Of course," he said, answering her question.

"I'll try to be careful," she said, turning a little toward him.

Her face was closer, but that didn't mean it was an invitation, only that it was more tempting. There was no smile, no dancing lights in her whiskey-colored eyes. "Rebecca," he said, fighting his desire with serious conversation, "the life of a soldier's wife can be difficult. Anything you think of that could make it easier, you're to tell me."

She smiled then, but moved away at the same time. "You forget," she said, taking a seat at the table, "this is how I grew up. This is the life I want."

He took the seat across from her. "I'm glad," he said, wondering if he really was. Knowing that she had intended to marry an officer and had found him as good as any other should make him feel better than thinking she hadn't wanted to marry at all.

She served the food and he ate, savoring the onion in the rice, complimenting her cooking. All the time he tried to decide how much he should take from her simple statement. If marriage to an officer, any officer, had been her plan all along, then he didn't need to feel she had made a sacrifice for him. She was in fact using him. That being the case, he should be able to use her as well without a twinge of guilt.

He glanced up at her as she delicately picked the meat from a bone. She noticed his scrutiny and grinned. "It's delicious, but messy."

He nodded in agreement, watching her suck the grease off the tip of a finger. He had kissed her before, and she hadn't been unwilling. A voice in the back of his mind told him that had been nothing more than a young girl's flirtation and was a far cry from what he was thinking.

He tried to ignore the voice. He wanted to believe he could forget yesterday's vow and demand his marital rights. She was his wife, whatever her reason had been.

"I was hoping you'd like it," she said.

Her face was a combination of eagerness and suspense. She reminded him of nothing so much as a little girl, awaiting praise for some special gift.

"It was perfect," he said, watching her face light with a smile that he swore seemed shy.

He was a fool. It was amazing what a man could talk himself into when the ache got bad enough. All she had meant was that she wanted to make the best of the situation. The meal proved how hard she was willing to work at it.

She stood to scrape the bones together and clear the table. He remained seated, watching her. Her movements were graceful, efficient. She caught him watching her again and gave him another shy smile.

He looked away quickly and came to his feet, helping her stack the dishes. He was finding himself as excited by her innocence as he had ever been by her flirting. How much more time could he spend with her before he forgot he was a gentleman? One more evening at least.

"You don't need to help," Rebecca said.

"I don't mind." They had both stopped and were gazing at each other.

"There aren't that many. It won't take me long."

"Even less if I help."

Her lips curled up in a tentative smile. "Are you afraid I'll break one of your mother's dishes?"

He thought he heard teasing in her voice. Her eyes seemed to hold a hint of a sparkle. But he didn't trust his perception tonight; he was too willing to believe what he wanted to.

"They *were* my mother's dishes," he said softly. "They're yours now."

She was still for a long moment. "Thank you," she murmured finally.

He had to turn away. "I'll heat some water," he said. He filled the kettle from the bucket and took it to the dying fire, scraped the hot coals together and set the kettle directly on them. He stayed outside until it was hot. Inside, he helped her with the dishes, trying not to watch her more than necessary.

Afterward he sat beside the lamp with his journal trying to forget that she sat near him, stitching a seam with the same light. He didn't look directly at her until she told him she was going to bed. He noticed a sadness about her eyes then that made him sure he had made the right decision.

Chapter Eleven

Rebecca sat on a camp chair in the middle of the tent, knowing she should be busy with something, but unable to think of anything that would really matter. Fatigue call sounded, calling the soldiers to their assigned tasks.

"What are my assigned tasks?" she muttered aloud. She should make the bed, find fresh flowers for the table and make plans for the evening meal.

She sighed. She had worked so hard yesterday, and the dinner had turned out well. Clark enjoyed it; she knew he did. Just not enough to warm his heart toward her. In fact, she had a feeling she made him uncomfortable.

She had even produced raisins for their oatmeal this morning. He had seemed surprised that they were available at the commissary. She would have liked to tell him that they hadn't even cost him a cent. She had traded back some of the salt pork for them, a trick she didn't expect to work a second time. She had fallen back on old habits and the sutler had been taken in by her dimpled smile. She was too ashamed to admit it to Clark.

Now she faced another day of trying to put together a great meal, knowing it would likely have no effect on her husband. She wouldn't mind cooking all day if she could anticipate a reward come nightfall. She hadn't expected yesterday's plan to fail. She had no alternate plan to fall back on.

"Mrs. Forrester?"

She recognized the Irish brogue of Paddy Malone. She stepped out of the tent to meet him.

"I brung ye three fine eggs today, ma'am," he said, taking them from various pockets.

Rebecca made a basket with her apron, and he laid them gently inside.

"Why aren't you on duty?" she asked.

"I've been hired as striker for the colonel. Gets me outa everythin' but guard duty and drill, only we don't drill on account o' no bein' built and all. And o'course, I could get called for actual patrol."

Rebecca smiled. "I thought Father already had a striker."

"He couldn't get along with the new lady."

Rebecca nodded her understanding. "Well, I hope you last longer," she said with a smile.

"I'll be doin' me best." He tipped his hat and left.

Rebecca laughed softly as she turned back toward the tent.

"Rebecca."

Clark's voice. She spun around to greet him, mindful of the fragile contents of her apron. He was right behind her.

"Eggs," she said, hoping to explain the meeting he had surely witnessed.

"Step inside," he said.

She did as she was told with some trepidation. She hoped he wasn't angry with her. But then that would mean he was jealous. He couldn't be jealous if he didn't care.

Instead of turning to speak to her he went to his trunk and began packing some things in a blanket roll. "I've been called out on patrol," he said. "A group of advance surveyors for the railroad came in. They had heard reports of raids in their area. We're to return them to their camp, leave a small detachment for their protection, and pursue the hostiles."

Rebecca stared in silence. He was leaving. Of course. He was a soldier. They were here for a reason. Yet somehow it hadn't occurred to her that he would leave, at least not so soon.

He turned and came toward her. "I shouldn't be gone more than a few days."

She couldn't think of anything to say. Her foolish mind wanted to find an excuse for him to stay.

He stopped beside her and kissed her cheek. "Save those eggs till I come back."

She didn't have time to react, to turn her head for a proper kiss. He was gone.

Save the eggs? She had forgotten the eggs. Her fist was frozen in the gathers of her apron. She stood a full minute before she shook off the shock enough to take the eggs to the crate of dishes and make a nest for them in the straw.

She wandered out of the tent, her mind in turmoil. He could be killed. She didn't remember ever worrying about her father, at least not like this. Why hadn't she thought of that? And what difference would it have made? She hadn't set out to fall in love with a soldier.

Near the corral she stopped to watch the men saddle their horses. It seemed like an awfully small force to send out. She would have liked to see at least two hundred men behind him instead of what? Thirty?

He had to come back. She hadn't told him she loved him, yet. *Please, God, don't let him get anywhere close to the Indians.*

She watched the lines form, watched Clark take his place at the head of the column. He saw her then and gave her a quick salute before he ordered the troops forward. She watched until the last of the line faded into the cloud of dust.

Hank came by late in the morning. "Rabbits, Mrs. Forrester," he said, holding the gruesome carcasses up proudly.

"Wonderful, Hank," Rebecca said, grabbing up an empty pan and holding it out so she wouldn't have to touch them.

He wiped his hands on his pants. "I'm curing the skins," he said.

She nodded, carrying the pan to a corner of the tent where she wouldn't have to look at it. She used to think hunting was so much fun.

"Might I have a dancing lesson now?"

"Yes, of course," she said, brightening. It was a perfect time. There was no danger of Clark interrupting them. She filled a basin with water and brought soap so Hank could wash. In a few minutes they had the table and chairs moved out of the way.

She stood in the middle of the tent and motioned Hank forward. He turned shy.

"Maybe you could just tell me how to do it."

Rebecca laughed. "I can tell you this, you can't dance with a girl without touching her. Come here."

"Yes, ma'am." He shuffled forward.

Rebecca spent an hour with Hank learning just how stiff and awkward a boy could be. When she didn't think her toes could stand another moment, she ended the lesson and sent him home. After soaking her bruised feet in cold water for a few minutes, she retrieved the pan with the rabbits and went to her father's tent.

She found Malone outside frying salt pork. "Will ye be joinin' the colonel's family for lunch, Mrs. Forrester?"

"I didn't realize it was noon," she said. "I brought some rabbits for supper."

He took the pan and grinned at her. "I suppose ye'll be wantin' a fine Irish stew."

She gave him a little curtsey. "That I would," she said with a touch of his accent. "Is the family inside?"

"I'd show ye in, but I reckon ye can find yer own way."

Alicia had heard her voice and came to the entrance to greet her with a hug. They moved farther into the tent arm in arm.

"Why aren't you home fixing lunch for your husband?" Aunt Belle asked.

"Clark's gone," Rebecca said.

"Gone? He's left you already."

"No." Leave it to Aunt Belle to think the worst. "He's left the fort. He's leading a troop of soldiers out to look for Indians."

Belle grunted as if that were merely an excuse. "I suppose you want to eat with us, then."

"Malone has already invited me," she said.

Belle's eyes narrowed. "How do you know our Paddy?"

Rebecca didn't want to give away Malone's secret.

"I met him yesterday," she said. "You should call him Malone."

"He's a servant. I'll call him Paddy." Belle took up the sewing she had set aside, dismissing the conversation.

Rebecca exchanged a smile with Alicia. She knew, even if the others didn't, what her father would say about that. "He's a soldier, still," she said, but Belle only shrugged.

"Is Father coming home for lunch?" Rebecca asked Alicia.

"I believe so. Come, let me show you what I'm making." Alicia led Rebecca out to the other tent. Inside she whispered, "How is everything? Rebecca, I still can't believe you're really married."

"Neither can I," she murmured. Seeing the concern on her cousin's face, she smiled. "Everything's just fine. He's really very sweet. And I'm going to surprise everyone and turn into a perfect housewife."

Alicia's look turned skeptical. "Don't change so much we don't know you."

Rebecca laughed. "It is a strain, I'll admit, but I have a couple of days before I have to come up with another fancy meal. Which isn't easy out here, by the way."

"But everything is all right? The lieutenant makes you happy?"

Alicia was watching her closely. Rebecca found she couldn't quite meet her eyes. "Everything's fine," she said again. "Now quick, show me what you're making in case your mother mentions it. I hear Father coming."

A moment later, they returned to the other tent. The colonel didn't appear surprised to see Rebecca. She assumed Belle had already informed him of her presence. An additional place had been set at the table.

"Well, Mrs. Forrester," he said by way of a greeting. "You look none the worse for wear."

"Levi!" admonished his sister. "What a thing to say."

The colonel only grinned. Rebecca had the sudden realization that he liked to shock Aunt Belle as much as she did.

"Speaking of which," she said, matching her father's grin, "did you have to send my husband away so soon after the wedding?"

The colonel frowned. "He volunteered," he said.

"Volunteered?" The word didn't seem to make sense.

The colonel nodded. "Ah, here's dinner. Let's sit down."

He led a quick blessing, and the food was passed. Levi and Belle had a brief discussion on the use of the striker's first name, though Malone swore he hadn't taken offense. Very little of it got through to Rebecca's one-track mind. Volunteered? He wanted to get away from her?

"You're not eating, Rebecca," her father said.

"What? Oh. I fixed such a big breakfast, I'm really not hungry." How easily the lies tripped off her tongue.

"Could it be a guilty conscience that's killed your appetite?"

She tried to laugh. "What are you talking about?"

Her father leveled a glare at her. "I'm talking about a new husband that willingly leaves his wife after only two nights. Have you denied him his marital rights?"

"Levi!" Belle leaned back in her chair, fanning her hot face with her napkin. "If this is the kind of conversation you've always had with your daughter, it's no wonder she's turned into such a...a... Oh!"

Levi ignored his sister. "Rebecca?"

Rebecca glanced around the table. Alicia stared wide-eyed, almost as horrified as her mother. Rebecca turned back to her father. We trapped poor Clark into this, you and I, she thought. But she wasn't sure she was up to that much honesty. Perhaps she simply wasn't *used* to honesty, at least not with her father.

She forced a smile. It wasn't so hard. She had had plenty of practice. "Don't be silly, Father," she said. "I haven't denied him anything. Perhaps he wanted a—rest."

There was another gasp from Belle, but neither Rebecca nor her father spared her a glance. She would have to swoon to get their attention, which was a real possibility. But for now Rebecca and her father stared at one another.

Finally the colonel nodded. "Don't mess this up, daughter."

"I'll try not to," she said with complete sincerity. "If you'll excuse me." She shared her smile with the women at the table. "I think I'll go home and—take a nap."

Aunt Belle groaned. Rebecca didn't wait to see if she actually fainted. She left the tent and hurried to her own. Inside, she lowered the flap, casting the small space in shadows. She slipped behind the canvas curtain and sank onto the bed. She wanted to give in to tears, but what good would that do? She needed a plan.

Ironically, the only thing she did well was tempt and tease. Clark had already seen all her tricks and knew them for what they were. If she greeted him with a sultry smile and told him she had missed him, he wouldn't believe she was sincere. In fact, he would probably assume she had been practicing the same flirtation on other men while he was gone.

There had to be another way. Could she pretend to be deathly ill? Would he realize her value if he were about to lose her? What if she tried to make him jealous?

She threw herself backward onto the bed with a

groan. Did her mind only understand subterfuge? Wasn't there an honest way to win a man?

She had already tried the only way she could think of, and it had failed. Or perhaps it simply took more time than she had given it. A cheerful, hardworking wife would ease the burdens of his life. Maybe it took years for gratitude to turn to love.

She rolled over and stifled a groan against the quilt. Years. And it was working so well so far that he had actually volunteered for patrol to get away from her.

She rolled back to a sitting position, her optimistic nature usurping her spell of fatalism. He was her husband. She loved him. She would think of something.

An hour later, Malone came to her tent. "Afternoon, Mrs. Forrester," he said slightly louder than was necessary. "'Tis just me stoppin' by to deliver a message to me employer's daughter."

"Thank you so much, Mr. Malone," she responded, taking the stack of blank writing paper he extended to her.

He looked to his right and left then slipped into the tent and lowered the flap. "Ye understand there's no message from the colonel. Just guardin' me secret."

"I understand." She lit a lamp and sat it on the table, taking a seat. "Sit down, Mr. Malone."

He did, after lowering the flame in the lamp a bit. "We'll be castin' shadows," he whispered.

Malone's very acts of secrecy were going to make things look even worse if they happened to be discovered. Still she could understand his feelings.

"Who are we writing to?" she asked, settling in for the task.

Thirty minutes later she had folded and sealed the letter, addressing it to New York. "I thought I'd be sending it to Ireland," she said.

"All me family's in America," he said with a touch of pride. "I joined the army 'cause it's hard ta find work."

Rebecca nodded her sympathy. "I'm willing to teach you to read, if you want. It could improve your chances at a better job."

He brushed the offer away with a grateful smile. "I'll be leavin' the paper here for next time, if ye don't mind," he said, sliding the letter into his pocket as he stood. "I'm much obliged."

He turned toward the entrance but hung back.

"Was there something else?" she asked.

"Could ye check ta see the coast is clear?"

Rebecca suppressed a smile. "Of course," she said. She raised the flap and stepped out, hearing him shuffle into the shadows behind her. "Looks good," she whispered.

He scooted around her quickly, touching his head

as if to tip a hat, and started away at a ground-eating walk.

Before he was out of sight, Aunt Belle came around the corner of a tent. Both she and Malone were startled to see the other. Malone recovered first, giving her a bow before moving on. Rebecca would have stepped back into the tent, but she was sure her aunt had already seen her. Trying to hide would only make things look worse.

"What did Paddy want?" Belle asked when she joined her.

"Oh, he was just passing by," Rebecca said.

"He hadn't been here to see you?"

Rebecca laughed. "Oh my, no. I had just stepped out when he walked by. We exchanged a greeting, that's all."

"Well," Belle said, turning to look in the direction Malone had taken. "You were standing here and he was hurrying away. You can imagine how it looked."

"Perhaps your imagination is better than mine," Rebecca said. "Have you come for tea?"

"That would be nice." She started into the tent then turned. "Why were you just standing here?"

"I was just going out," Rebecca said, reaching for the kettle. "I understand there's a farmer not far from the fort who has goats. I thought I might try to make a deal for some milk."

"Goat's milk?" Belle looked queasy.

Rebecca decided not to argue. "I thought it might be better than nothing."

Belle waved the idea away. "I wouldn't be leaving the fort anyway. From what your father said, those surveyors weren't camped very far from here. The Indians must be close."

It was easy to agree not to go. She didn't need the milk anyway with Clark gone. She had wanted it for his coffee, for his oatmeal, maybe for some custard if she got enough eggs. What did she care about any of those things for herself?

When the kettle was on the rekindled fire, Rebecca followed Belle into the tent. "Why didn't Alicia come with you?" she asked.

"She's napping. She doesn't sleep well. But who does on those awful cots?"

Rebecca was sure her face showed no more than the appropriate concern. "Does she get up and move around at night?"

"You mean like a sleepwalker? Of course not."

Rebecca shook her head. "I'm only suggesting that a little exercise might help her. And if the cot is truly uncomfortable for her, moving around a little can ease the stiffness. It was just a thought."

Of course it wasn't at all what she was thinking. But if Alicia was still sneaking out to meet Brooks, her mother was evidently unaware of it. Rebecca clung to that bit of information and tried to relax.

The first chance she got, she would talk to Alicia alone.

After about fifteen minutes of mindless chatter, Rebecca began to wonder why Belle had come. She knew she wasn't Belle's first choice for a companion. The woman didn't seem to have anything in particular she wanted to tell her or ask of her. Had the unannounced visit been a way of checking up on her?

By the time Belle left nearly half an hour later, Rebecca was sure of it. And since Belle naturally thought the worst, she was probably convinced there was something going on between Rebecca and Malone.

What difference did it make? She slipped back into her seat and stared at the empty teacups. It wasn't as if a rumor like that was going to break Clark's heart.

One lonely day slipped into two, then three. Hank came by each morning with more meat, which she took to her father's tent after the dance lesson. She didn't have the heart to tell the boy she didn't want the meat until Clark came home.

Malone hadn't been back either with eggs or to write another letter. She knew he had other customers for the eggs and suspected she wouldn't get any more until he got an answer to his letter.

Powers had yet to bring her any mending. She felt guilty but not enough to approach him about it. She had been by the corral a couple of times and knew her horse was well cared for.

She got up and moved her chair deeper into the shade of the tent. The days had grown hotter and the only relief seemed to be to find a place in the shade that caught the breeze. Tomorrow, she reminded herself, would be the first day of July. It was supposed to be hot.

Today was Sunday. The noise around the camp had a more disorganized air. It rose and fell occasionally. Now it seemed to be somewhat on the rise. Rebecca had no interest in investigating the cause. It was too easy to sit and do nothing.

Earlier, the chaplain had led an open-air service. She had attended, of course. It was expected, and there was nothing else to do.

That wasn't entirely true. There were things she could be doing, like finding Powers. There was no fatigue duty on Sundays which made it a perfect time to look for him.

She could ride her horse, though the thought of riding in skirts wasn't appealing. She had been spoiled by the pants.

She could invite Alicia over and try, yet again, to find out what was bothering her. Rebecca frowned. Alicia was keeping something from her. She swore she wasn't meeting Brooks, but the subject made her nervous. Maybe one more try would bring out the truth.

Yes, she decided. That was what she would do. Soon. She stared into the cloudless sky. How could she concentrate on Alicia when all she thought about was Clark?

She closed her eyes and let her imagination have free rein as she did so often lately. She missed him more than she ever would have imagined. Even his cool distance was better than his absence. At least when he was around she could watch him. And she definitely liked that. She liked to watch him ride, to watch him walk. To watch him shave.

And his voice. That deep, masculine voice with the charming accent. And when he dropped his voice just above a whisper, he could send tremors through her body.

"Rebecca?"

Yes, just like that. Her imagination was better than she thought. She could have sworn she had heard him. She sighed contentedly.

"Rebecca."

Her eyes flew open. Clark was kneeling beside her chair. She stopped just short of throwing herself into his arms.

"I didn't know you were back," she said, unnecessarily.

He smiled. "We made a small commotion, but it appears you were asleep."

"I guess so. How did everything go?" she asked,

hoping to distract him before he asked why she had been smiling in her sleep.

"The surveyors have been returned to their camp with some soldiers left to guard them. We checked out the reports but never saw any Indians. Just rumors, I guess."

"I can't say I'm sorry."

"I doubt if your father will feel the same way. I need to report. And get cleaned up. We can talk more at supper."

She watched him rise and walk away, letting herself smile again. He was home. A tiny spark of hope ignited in her heart. He had come to see her first.

But the smile lasted only a moment. Supper. She sat back and groaned. Well, she had some time to come up with something. She didn't want to think that giving her time to start supper was the only reason Clark had come to her first. She got up and took the chair with her into the tent.

Opal didn't allow Hank to hunt on Sundays so there would be no fresh meat. She wanted to fix something better than the salt pork Clark had been eating while he was gone. She looked through her supply of food. Beans needed to soak overnight. She wanted to save the eggs for breakfast.

She didn't have much choice, she decided. Maybe some cornbread would make up for the salt pork. She had half the ingredients mixed before she realized she would have to use one of the eggs.

"Fine," she muttered, choosing the smallest of the three. "I won't have one tomorrow."

She added the water and beat the batter until it was smooth. She reached for a pan and realized she didn't know how to bake it over an open fire.

There was probably time to run and ask Opal. She tossed a cloth over her batter and hurried to her friend's tent. Opal's instructions were specific and detailed, but it was nearly thirty minutes later before Rebecca returned to her tent.

She had poured the batter into the small deep skillet Opal loaned her when she heard a knock on a tent post.

"Mrs. Forrester?"

"Yes, Hank." She put the lid on the skillet and went to the tent entrance.

Hank grinned at her. "Catfish."

"Bless you, Hank!" Rebecca laughed, delighted. They were already cleaned, and he carried them in a bucket for once. "I didn't expect you today."

"Fishin' ain't huntin'," he said. "Can we dance? I already washed."

Rebecca hesitated. How long before Clark came home for dinner? The fish would fry quickly; surely there was time. And if he caught them dancing? Would he be jealous? The urge to find out overruled her common sense.

"Sure, Hank," she said, smiling. "But I need to get my cornbread baking first."

"I can help, ma'am," the boy said.

He did more than help. In a surprisingly short time, he had the skillet resting on hot coals in an impression near the fire with a few more coals on top of the lid.

He stood up, brushing off his hands. "Do you know how to fry the fish?"

"I think I can manage," Rebecca said.

Hank grinned. "Then let's dance."

He helped her move the table aside then shook out his arms as if limbering up for some test of strength. He took her hand and put his other hand gently on her waist—and stepped on her toe.

"I'm awful sorry, Mrs. Forrester," he moaned.

"Hank, the reason you step on a girl's toes is because she can't guess where you're going."

"Well, how could she guess that when I don't even know?"

"You need to know, Hank," she said. "You need to decide on a reasonable pattern and stick to it. I wouldn't try anything fancy."

"Yes, ma'am."

He started again. Rebecca hummed a slow tune, designed as much to make Hank relax as to serve as rhythm for dancing. After a few minutes he seemed to get the hang of it. She could predict that he would take two steps forward then turn to the side and managed to keep her toes out from under his.

After several minutes she ended the tune and stepped away from him. "Very good, Hank."

"It was good, wasn't it? I was starting to think I wouldn't never learn."

Rebecca had been sure of it. "Of course, you'll learn, Hank."

"I really appreciate the dancin' and all," he said, backing toward the tent entrance. "I'll see you tomorrow, ma'am." He nodded to her and backed directly into Clark.

"Sorry, sir," he said, spinning around. "Excuse me. Ah, night, ma'am. Sir." He practically turned and fled.

Clark came into the tent, one eyebrow raised. "Let me guess. Your mighty hunter?"

"Major Raymond's son, Hank." Two minutes sooner and he could have seen his wife in the mighty hunter's arms. Sort of. Would she have gotten more than a raised eyebrow then?

She dismissed the thought, disgusted with herself. What kind of wife tried to make her husband jealous? Still she couldn't help thinking it would indicate some degree of interest, which he didn't seem to display otherwise.

She realized she was still standing in the middle of the tent. Clark was eyeing the table that had been moved out of the way. *Ask me why it's there.* But he didn't.

"Here, let's move that back," she said, stepping

to his side. He smelled of soap and reminded her suddenly of the evening after the burned homestead. He had been so sweet to her that evening. She remembered how he had touched her cheek—and how he hadn't kissed her. She should have been paying more attention. He had been trying to tell her even then that he had no desire for her.

"Rebecca?"

She looked up sharply. Clark had lifted the table, and she was standing in his way. "Sorry," she said, moving aside. "I'll put the fish on."

"Fish? From the Raymond boy?"

Rebecca busied herself with preparing the skillet. "He brought them by just now."

There he had it. If there had been any uncertainty she had just eased his mind. There was nothing to be jealous about. In fact, he could apologize for harboring such thoughts. She glanced in his direction. He was positioning the chairs beside the table.

Without another word she took the skillet out to the fire. How hard did she have to be hit over the head? He wasn't jealous. He hadn't caught them dancing, but even if he had, he wouldn't have cared. Hank was, after all, just a boy. It wasn't a good test of Clark's feelings.

And she shouldn't be testing them anyway. Though what she should be doing, she had no idea.

She heard Clark come up behind her. "Can I help?" he asked.

"If you'll watch the fish, I'll check the corn-bread." The sizzling fish gave her an excuse not to look at him.

"All right," he said, crouching close beside her.

She inhaled his scent along with the wood smoke. The temptation to turn into his arms was too great, and she moved away.

The cornbread looked done on top but she worried about the center. She replaced the lid and hoped it would continue cooking a little even without the coals on top. With nothing else to do while the fish cooked, she sat back on her heels and watched Clark.

He had fried fish before. With a combination of shaking and prodding, he kept the fish from sticking to the pan. He watched them intently, keeping them in just the right amount of heat, oblivious to her presence.

His profile gave her a perfect view of his jaw. Her fingers itched to trace the long, lean line. He hadn't shaved since his return, though she could guess he had shaved that morning. The firelight cast the dark hairs in relief, tempting her fingers even more.

"Did you bathe in the creek?" Rebecca bit her lip. How could thoughts slip out of her mouth without asking permission?

"Yes," he said without turning. "I think I traded prairie dust for creek mud, but it was refreshing."

This subject overstimulated her imagination. And it was purely imagination, though she had seen him without his shirt a couple of times. She should ask something else, change the subject. The trouble was, her imagination wouldn't allow her to think about anything else.

"Would you like to?"

Lord, yes! "Like to what?" she croaked.

"Like to go for a swim. I'd guard your privacy."

Her mind went racing over the possibilities. Alone. At twilight. And she would be naked.

"Yes," she said.

Chapter Twelve

Clark regretted his offer almost immediately. The innocent girl was trusting him to protect her, and he was having lustful thoughts before she even removed a stitch of clothing. How was he going to stand by and watch her bathe? By not watching, he decided.

She brought the plates for the fish, and he followed her into the tent with the skillet of cornbread. Maybe if he stalled long enough, it would get dark. It wouldn't be safe to swim in the dark. Surely her father had a washtub or something she could borrow. She could take her bath tomorrow while he was gone. And too busy to think about it.

No. He would never be that busy.

He glanced at Rebecca as he took his seat at the table. She smiled, pleased with the prospect of a bath. He hated to disappoint her.

Perhaps a discussion on the current Indian troubles would put her in the mood to stay home. "Governor

Crawford's been authorized to enlist a volunteer cavalry," he said.

She cut out a chunk of the cornbread and passed it to him. "I thought General Sherman was against it for fear of another Sand Creek."

Clark nodded. "They won't be allowed to campaign on their own. They'll be under the command of the regular army."

"Does the situation warrant more troops?"

"I'm afraid so," he said. "I understand Fort Wallace was virtually under siege last week. They got reinforcements from Custer's troops, which leaves him fewer men. Pond Creek Station has been struck twice now. Captain Barnitz took a company out after them this last time, and the Indians turned and charged squadron style. Seven soldiers were killed."

"That's unusual, isn't it?"

"Extremely. The same Indians attacked a supply train headed for Custer's camp on the Republican."

"The volunteers will at least put more men in the field."

Clark nodded his agreement. It seemed a shame to ruin a nice meal with such grim reports. Somehow he had expected her to be less interested and more frightened. He should have known better.

"Will you be going out again?" she asked.

"That depends on your father. He wants the barracks up by winter, and every soldier on patrol means one less carpenter for the fort."

She lapsed into silence. He watched her while he ate. She was thoughtful. Had he discouraged her?

"Did you ever find out about the family we found?" she asked after a few minutes.

"Yes." If she had laid her hand on the table he would have settled his on top of it. "They only had the one child."

She nodded solemnly. He could guess what she was thinking. There was no little child suffering captivity. There was no hope of a child to return to grandparents who had lost so much.

They had made short work of the meal, and Clark thought Rebecca's mood was sufficiently melancholy. "Do you still want to go to the creek?" he asked gently.

She looked up, her face slowly brightening. "Yes. You knew just what would cheer me up."

Clark thought he should be disappointed, but her smile made it impossible. "Get your things together. We'll want to be back before dark." When she hesitated, he added, "I'll clean up here."

She jumped up and ran to her trunk. He tried not to notice the frilly white garments she was sorting through. He went in search of a cloth to cover the remaining cornbread as a way of turning his back.

"I've been meaning to ask," she said. "Among all this camp gear, why do you have your mother's china?"

"I brought it back on the train," he said, scraping

the fish bones together. "When my mother died, her sister took the china. Now my aunt's husband is gone, and she's moving in with her youngest daughter."

"And the family wanted you to have your mother's china?"

Clark paused a moment before answering. "My aunt wanted me to have it, more from loyalty to my mother's memory than any love for me."

She turned to look at him, and he wondered if he had said more than he should have. "But you also got your uncle's chess set."

"Yes. But I understand that had been among his last requests. And even then it wasn't without opposition." It was amazing to him how his cousins drew up battle lines where he was concerned.

"Families," Rebecca said, with a touch of the south on the vowels. "Aren't they just wonderful?"

Clark laughed. She went back to gathering her clothes, and he took the bones out and scraped them into the dying fire. He was grateful to Rebecca for making him laugh. He had few reasons to smile without her in his life.

He carried the plate back to the table to stack it with the others and found Rebecca waiting, a large bundle in her arms. "I can wash the dishes by lamplight when we come back," she said. "Let's go."

He took a minute to slide everything off his utility

belt except the gun holster and strapped it on. "Can I help you carry anything?"

"I can't share this load without dropping something," she said. "Just lead me to the creek."

With one arm hovering near her back ready to steady her if she stumbled on the uneven ground, he walked slowly toward Big Creek. In the heat of the day the trees along the bank had been inviting. Now, with this woman at his side, he thought of snakes and concealed predators of the four- and two-legged varieties. Bringing Rebecca here seemed like a bad idea.

He reminded himself of how good the cool water had felt on his parched skin, but picturing Rebecca having the same pleasure made his body hotter than it had been in the heat of the day.

At the creek he led her through the trees to the spot he had found. The bottom of the stream was a slab of rock, making it possible to wash without standing ankle-deep in mud. Rebecca placed her bundle far enough from the water to stay dry and sat down on a log. She hiked her skirts up to her knees and bent to remove her shoes.

Clark looked away. "I'll scout around a little and make sure nobody else is nearby."

He congratulated himself on his quick thinking. He could probably make this last a good ten minutes. Within five minutes, he found himself hurrying back to Rebecca. There was no sign of anyone else in the area, but he felt uncomfortable leaving her alone.

He found her standing in water up to her thighs. She had taken off every stitch of clothing. Somehow he had expected her to leave something on. That was foolish, he realized, if she planned to wash. Still, he thought she'd be more inhibited.

And she probably would be if she turned and caught him staring at her. But he couldn't help it. The pants she had worn had given away the sweet curve of her hips but hadn't completely prepared him for how her soft bottom looked clad only in creamy skin and soap bubbles. It made him long to know what her breasts looked like.

One careful step to his right revealed a hint of curve when she raised her arm. He tried to control his breathing which was getting dangerously close to panting, but his racing heart made it difficult. It was a wonder she didn't hear him.

She bent over and lifted handfuls of water to rinse the soap from her legs, and he saw her breast in perfect profile. Water dripped from the puckered nipple. The tension in his gut tightened another notch.

She splashed water over the rest of her body, and he realized he was getting a better view of her round breasts and flat stomach. Had he been moving without knowing it? He tore his eyes away from the vision that was his wife and studied the rest of his surroundings. No. He was sure he was standing where the sight of her had stopped him. Except for that one calculated step, of course.

She had turned. Was still turning. He could glimpse the dark nest between her legs. Was she turning to avoid some breeze that chilled her wet skin? He would welcome a hint of the same breeze! When she turned one step too far and saw him staring at her, would she scream?

He should step back. He should turn away. And he would. In just a second.

"Clark?"

Her voice brought his head up. At least she hadn't screamed. He tried to swallow, but his mouth had gone dry. He didn't even try to speak.

"Could you bring me the towel?"

He watched her walk to the edge of the stream and stop, her tiny feet balancing on a rock on the bank. He must have stared at her for a full minute. The towel. He could bring it to her. His body seemed unable to respond except in lust.

He willed himself to move. He wasn't an animal. He didn't need to give in to every urge. He was, or used to be, a gentleman.

However, he was not, as she seemed to think, made of stone. He brought her the towel, nearly tossed it to her, and turned away. Or tried to.

"Clark?"

He turned back, trying desperately to keep his eyes on her face. Why didn't she use the towel to cover herself? All she seemed interested in drying was her hair.

"Could you carry me up the bank? I'm afraid I'll slip in the mud and be dirtier than when I started."

It made a kind of sense. If you discounted the lustful thoughts brewing in his head.

He took a step closer, mindful of his own footing. He started to reach around her and changed his mind. He pulled the towel out of her hands. She gave it up with some surprise. He wrapped the small piece of cloth around her, then scooped her into his arms.

The towel hadn't been as helpful as he had hoped. Both hands managed to encounter bare skin, and the towel dropped to the ground when he set her on her feet. It took her forever to pick it up. But it took him even longer to turn away.

With his back to her the fog in his brain started to lift, even though the ache remained. He tried to think of sobering events, his uncle's funeral, his aunt's scorn, the burned-out homestead, older memories of carnage. His brain dismissed them as unimportant. Instead it pictured Rebecca, rubbing the towel over her pink skin, drying the dark nipples. She seemed intent on encouraging his imagination. She hummed as she dressed.

He didn't trust his guess of how much time had passed when she stepped up beside him. She touched his arm. "Thanks," she said.

He couldn't bring himself to answer beyond a

grunt of acknowledgement. He started toward the fort, unwilling to risk touching her. He shouldn't blame her. Though he had trouble believing she was so innocent she didn't know better than to undress in front of a man.

Or perhaps she had stood naked in front of so many men it didn't even bother her. She hadn't seemed the least self-conscious. And her behavior since he'd met her had bordered on brazen.

"Clark, you're making me run."

With a steadying sigh, he slowed his steps. But he didn't dare look at her. He would be too tempted to shake some sense into her. Or better yet, kiss her senseless.

What kind of game was she playing? Was she testing him? He'd love to believe she was deliberately tempting him, but he had seen her flirtatious smiles, knew she wouldn't hesitate to make the first move if she wanted a kiss.

No, this had been something different. Extreme innocence. Or deliberate torture. Knowing what he did about Rebecca, he would put his money on torture. Though if that was the case, she had made quite a gamble. Unless she didn't realize how hard it was for a man to resist such accessible temptation.

"Clark!" This time she grabbed his arm and he stopped. "Why are you in such a hurry?"

"It's been a long day," he said, barely looking at her. They were on the edge of the camp, and he considered going on without her. Instead, he took her arm and urged her forward, trying to keep his own pace reasonably slow. At the tent entrance he dropped her arm.

"I have a few things I need to check on." He left her before she had a chance to respond. He would walk it off. Or take another dunk in the creek. And make sure he didn't come back until she was sound asleep.

Rebecca debated whether she should go to bed or spend the whole night sitting in a chair feeling sorry for herself. Probably the latter. Clark had seen everything she had to offer and had rejected her. He hadn't even come home.

One lantern burned low on the table and she stared at it. She was ashamed of her behavior. Perhaps he was as well. In fact she was sure of it. No well-bred woman would have done what she did. Clearly, he had been angry with her on their return.

But she had wanted him to find her attractive, perhaps even irresistible. All she had done was prove her father right when he accused her of being manipulative.

She thought again about going to bed. She didn't really want to face Clark when he came in. Yet sitting up seemed a kind of penance for what she had done. She didn't deserve the luxury of the soft bed since she had driven her husband from it.

Her husband. He wasn't truly that, was he? The marriage could easily be dissolved until it was consummated. A sudden revelation made her breath catch in her throat. Perhaps that was why he wouldn't touch her. When he was transferred away from her father, he could divorce her.

With a stab of sorrow she decided it would be for the best. She couldn't spend her life longing for him and never feeling his touch. How unfair that she should love a man who didn't love her!

She was trying to decide what images to punish herself with next, when she heard something outside. Her first thought was Clark had finally returned, but an instant later she knew it wasn't him. She turned up the flame on the lantern and carried it to the front of the tent. Lifting the flap cautiously, she peered out. The light fell on a pile of dirty cloth and a mass of pale blond hair.

"Alicia!" Rebecca nearly dropped the lantern as she ran to her cousin's side. Alicia raised her head. Blood caked one side of her face and hair and oozed from a corner of her mouth. She was shaking and gasping for breath as if she had been crying hysterically.

"Alicia, what happened?"

Alicia dropped her face back into the dirt.

"Come on, sweetheart." Rebecca urged Alicia to her feet. With one arm wrapped around her and the other holding the lantern, she led her into the tent. "Sit down, I'll get the doctor."

"No!" Alicia clutched Rebecca's hand. "Don't leave me."

Alicia's legs were shaking. Rebecca led her past the chair and settled her onto the bed. She tried to loosen Alicia's grip on her hand. "Let me get some water to wash your face."

"No!" Alicia broke into heaving sobs.

"All right," she soothed. "It's all right. I won't leave you." She set the lantern on the floor at her feet. It cast bizarre shadows that made Alicia look even worse. "Sweetheart, just relax."

When the sobbing stopped she ventured to ask again, "What happened?"

Alicia just shook her head.

"Someone hurt you. Tell me."

Alicia swallowed, then made a croaking sound.

"Alicia?"

"Victor." Tears streamed from her eyes and mingled with the blood.

Rebecca had to choke down her fury in order to speak. She tried her best to keep her voice calm for Alicia's sake. "Victor Brooks did this to you?"

"It was my fault," Alicia sobbed.

Like hell. "Honey, how could this be your fault?"

"I shouldn't have g-g-gone to meet him."

Hearing the girl's voice get caught on a sob brought tears to Rebecca's eyes. "That doesn't make this your fault, Alicia. He hurt you. Oh, Alicia. Did he—?''

Alicia's cry of anguish was all the answer she needed. She wanted to kill him. Of course, she couldn't go search for the bastard until Alicia released her hand. Where was Clark?

While she waited, maybe she could get some information that would help them find him. "Tell me what happened, honey. Where were you? Do you know where he went?"

Alicia shook her head. "He's been sending me notes. I didn't want to see him again. He hurt me once before."

"The night you said you fell."

Alicia nodded. "His notes got worse. More threatening. Tonight it said he'd hurt you if I didn't come."

"You should have told Father about the notes."

Alicia's voice dropped so low Rebecca had to lean forward to hear. "I was afraid he would make me marry him."

Rebecca cursed herself. The notes. They were the reason for Alicia's sleeplessness. And she might have gotten the information out of Alicia this afternoon if she hadn't been so lazy and wrapped up in herself. She took a deep breath. "So you went to meet him tonight. Where?"

"Near the construction site. I told him I didn't want him sending any more notes. I wasn't going to see him again. He—" She broke into sobs again.

"It's all right, Alicia. You don't have to say any more. Just be still. I'm here."

"Rebecca?"

"Clark! I'm so glad you're home."

He came around the curtain and stared in disbelief. "My God."

"Get the doctor," Rebecca said as calmly as she could. With Clark here she had a sudden urge to fall apart. "Get Father and tell him to arrest Victor Brooks."

Without a word, Clark was gone. She had to be strong for Alicia, she told herself. The poor girl was sobbing again. "Hush now, sweetheart. It's going to be all right."

"Everyone will know," Alicia sobbed. "Uncle Levi will make me ma—ma—" The rest of what she might have said was buried in her sobs.

"No. No, sweetheart. Father isn't that cruel. He'll make them hang him." She hoped it was true. Of course they had to catch him first and her instinct told her the bastard was long gone.

Rebecca stroked Alicia's hair, the side that wasn't bloody, until the sobbing subsided. Alicia's eyes were closed and Rebecca might have thought she was asleep except for the strong grip she still felt on her hand.

A dull light glowed through the tent wall and Rebecca called, "Doctor?"

"Dr. Garman," he said. He came slowly around the curtain, carrying a lantern which he held high in one hand. "You must be Mrs. Forrester. And this must be our Alicia."

Rebecca wasn't sure his presence was reassuring. He looked like he was a hundred years old. Of course the lanterns weren't exactly casting flattering shadows.

He moved around to the side of the bed away from Rebecca and sat down, still holding his lantern. "We have some cuts to wash, don't we, dear? Are you bleeding anywhere else?"

Alicia shook her head.

"Now, little girl, I'm going to have to ask you some questions no proper lady should ever have to hear, but I can't help you until I know. Can you understand?"

Rebecca had raised her eyebrow at her cousin being called a little girl. Surely tonight's events had forced her to grow up if nothing else had. But Alicia only watched the doctor's face and slowly nodded.

"A man did this to you." He almost touched the cut on her forehead. "Am I right?"

Another nod.

"And this." His hand hovered above the cut lip. "Did he also force himself on you?"

Alicia's face puckered up to cry again, but she managed a tiny nod.

Rebecca glared at the doctor. She could have told the fool that.

"Are you bleeding there, child?"

Alicia only sobbed.

"I need to check."

"No!" Alicia turned pleading eyes toward Rebecca.

"I'll check," Rebecca said. She lifted the lantern from the floor and gently pulled her hand out of Alicia's grasp. Alicia sobbed louder when Rebecca raised her skirts and gently lifted one of her knees.

"No blood," she reported to the doctor. She smoothed the skirt over Alicia's legs and moved back to her former place. Alicia reached out to her, and she let her take her hand again. She couldn't forget the sight of Alicia's torn pantalets and the bruises on her thighs.

"Well." Dr. Garman gave her a reassuring smile. "That's good then. I'd like a closer look at these cuts."

"Alicia!" The call came from outside the tent.

"Uncle Levi," Alicia gasped.

"I'll take care of him," Rebecca soothed, easing her hand away. "You tell the doctor about the cuts and anything else that hurts."

Taking her lantern with her she slipped around the curtain. Her father let himself into the tent "You're going to raise the entire camp," she hissed.

"Where is she?" At least his voice had dropped a little.

"She's in bed. The doctor's with her."

"Was Clark right? Has she been—?"

Rebecca nodded. "She'll be all right. We just need

to keep her calm. I think she ought to stay here with me tonight.''

Rebecca watched her father pace across the tent, and thought how odd and yet familiar it was. "I suppose you're right," he said. "If I take her home I'll just have two hysterical women on my hands."

Rebecca thought that was a rather selfish analysis of the situation. She might have said so, but Clark came into the tent. "He's gone, sir," he said.

The colonel stopped in front of him. "Horse and gear with him, I imagine."

"Yes, sir."

"Take out a small detachment in the morning and bring the deserter back. Not one word of this," he pointed at the curtain, "to anyone. Understood?"

"Of course, sir."

"I'm going home," he said, turning toward Rebecca. "I don't want Belle to wake up and find herself alone. If there's anything I can do, let me know."

He left the tent before Rebecca could respond. She took a step toward Clark. "Is he in more trouble for deserting than for raping an innocent girl?"

"Your father's trying to protect her."

Rebecca sighed. "I'm sorry," she whispered. Clark's strong arms wrapped around her, and his shoulder cradled her head. She felt herself ready to give into tears.

"May I have a word with you?"

She jerked out of Clark's arms at the doctor's voice. "What is it? Is she all right?"

The doctor nodded. "I think so. We have to worry about the possibility of a baby. And I'd like the man examined for any sign of disease."

Rebecca wanted to turn back into Clark's shoulder. She hadn't considered either of these.

"I'm leaving a powder that will help her sleep," the doctor continued. "I suggest you get her cleaned up. She'll be more comfortable."

Rebecca thanked the doctor as he tottered toward the door.

"I'll heat some water," Clark offered. "You ladies may have the tent."

"Where will you sleep?" She didn't want him gone. He had been gone so long, and now he was leaving again in the morning. But she needed to be with Alicia.

"I'll be right outside."

"I'm sorry, Clark. You should get to sleep in a bed when you're home."

"Shhh." His fingertips touched her lips. "I'll be fine. And I won't be far if you need me."

She took comfort in that knowledge while she prepared the washtub for Alicia to stand in. After Clark had added the hot water and bade her good-night, she washed her cousin, gave her the powder and tucked her into bed.

Finally she stretched out beside Alicia, conscious that she was on Clark's side of the bed. And he was outside. And this wasn't at all the way she wanted it.

Chapter Thirteen

Rebecca awoke the next morning certain that Clark was already gone. She had overslept but it hardly mattered. Clark had probably gotten an early start, and once he was gone, what difference did it make if she slept the day away? Alicia looked ready to do just that.

But Alicia had the powder to help her sleep. Rebecca was soon feeling restless and crawled out of bed. While she was reviving the fire to make some coffee, she had a visitor.

"Sergeant Whiting," she said, reaching out to shake his hand. "What brings you here this morning?"

"The lieutenant asked me to check in on you and Miss Evans while he was gone."

Rebecca couldn't hide her surprise.

"I'm sure he meant no disrespect, ma'am. He told

me your cousin's staying with you because you had gotten worried last time he was gone.''

Rebecca decided not to destroy a perfect excuse. For a moment she had thought Clark might have told Whiting about the attack. "Time passes so slowly when I'm alone. Alicia will help keep me occupied. Can you stay for coffee?"

"My pleasure, ma'am."

Rebecca put the coffee on and settled into one of the camp chairs. "It's a pretty morning," she said, hoping to explain why she was remaining outside the tent.

"It is, ma'am." He took the other chair. "Gonna be a hot one, though."

"Sergeant," Rebecca asked, smiling so he wouldn't take offence, "why aren't you on duty?"

"Sick list," he answered, sliding up his sleeve to reveal a white bandage. "I was working on the barracks and a board slipped. It's festering a little. Doc took me off duty but turned me out of the hospital tent. I look on it as a vacation."

"The doctor's still watching it, isn't he?"

"Oh, yeah. I'm supposed to go see him every day. The rest of the time, I'm free to roam the fort. Somebody's gonna get wise to the fact that I can still perform my duties and countermand Doc's orders. I figure I got two days tops unless I can contrive to run a fever."

Rebecca tried to look serious. "I should report you, soldier."

Whiting nodded. "That you should, ma'am. 'Cept who would come by and see that you and your cousin are all right?"

"Well, sir," Rebecca said, "I'm not sure I need your concern, but I appreciate your company. And any news you might have."

"I'll keep my ears open," he promised. "Your coffee's ready. I'll toss in some cold water to settle the grounds while you see if your little cousin wants to join us."

Rebecca thanked him and entered the tent. It took a moment for her eyes to adjust to the dark. When they did, she saw Alicia hovering near the canvas curtain. She looked like a frightened little child.

"Alicia," Rebecca said, just above a whisper, "do you want to come out and have breakfast?"

"Is he gone?"

"It's just Sergeant Whiting."

Alicia shook her head. "I can't. My dress is torn. And look at my face."

Of course. If Alicia was going to keep her attack a secret, she couldn't very well step outside the tent in a torn dress with bright cuts visible on her pale face. "I'll bring you a cup. You can have it with some cornbread."

She took three cups out to the fire. "Alicia needs her cup of coffee before she's ready to meet anyone," she offered as an excuse. Whiting seemed to accept it readily enough.

Inside, Alicia had helped herself to a chunk of the cornbread, and Rebecca traded her the cup for the pan. Between bites, Whiting talked about the construction and his own assessment of when the fort would be completed.

Rebecca was laughing at one of Whiting's remarks when she caught sight of her aunt bearing down on them. The woman was not in the mood for humor.

Whiting must have read Rebecca's expression because he turned to see what had caught her attention. "Good morning, Mrs. Evans," he said, standing.

Aunt Belle didn't acknowledge the greeting but demanded, "Where is she?"

Before Rebecca could answer, Whiting handed his cup to her. "It's been a pleasure, ma'am."

As he beat a hasty retreat, Aunt Belle swept aside the flap. "I'll just bet," she tossed over her shoulder as she entered the tent.

Rebecca was right behind her. "What is that supposed to mean?"

Belle didn't seem to hear. "Alicia! Levi told me what happened. How could you be so foolish?"

Alicia sat at the table, the cup frozen halfway to her mouth. Rebecca ran to her rescue. With her hands on the girl's shoulders she faced her aunt. "This wasn't Alicia's fault."

Belle's eyes narrowed. "No, I suppose not. She has you to blame for it."

Rebecca didn't care what Belle said as long as she didn't yell at Alicia. She gently squeezed the girl's shoulders hoping to reassure her.

Alicia slowly returned the cup to the saucer and folded her hands in her lap. "Rebecca didn't do anything, Mother."

"Well, of course she did. Her husband has just left and already she's entertaining another man. This has been your example since she came to live with us."

"Mother—"

Rebecca spoke up. "Hush, Alicia. It's all right. Clark asked Sergeant Whiting to check in on us."

"He can continue to check in on *you* all he wants. But Alicia is coming with me."

Alicia shrank back against Rebecca.

"Let her stay," Rebecca said. "You have my father's household to run and the other duties of your station. Here she won't be alone while she waits for the cuts to heal. And you can simply tell anyone who asks that she's keeping me company. She can go back when Clark gets home."

Belle eyed Alicia critically, probably assessing the damage that would be done if anyone saw her. Finally she gave in. "Come over later and get her clothes. But see you don't ruin her reputation along with your own."

The woman was on her way out when Hank presented himself holding four plucked prairie chickens aloft. Belle gave him the once-over and grunted as she turned away.

Hank's usual enthusiasm was sadly dampened by the woman's reaction. Rebecca gave the boy her warmest smile. "Oh, look what you have today! Alicia, won't these taste wonderful?"

Rebecca was glad to see Hank smile again, but she got no response from Alicia. A glance over her shoulder showed the seat by the table to be empty. Alicia had retreated to the bedroom.

"If you'll get that bucket, I'll wash my hands. Then I can show you what I been practicin'."

In a moment Hank was ready to start the dancing lesson. Rebecca tried to ignore her worry for her cousin as she danced with Hank. He really had come a long way from their first lesson. He even added his baritone to Rebecca's alto, humming part of the time.

Before he left, he helped Rebecca open the front of the tent to let in a breeze. The part that formed a wall of the bedroom, they left in place, providing Alicia with a sanctuary.

While Rebecca was trying to coax Alicia out of the bedroom to get some air, Powers knocked on the tent post. He carried a bushel basket.

"I was wondering when you'd let me start repaying you," she said as she went to greet him.

"Your horse is doing fine, ma'am," he said, handing her the basket. The clothes looked freshly laundered.

"I'll have these done as soon as I can," she said. The task looked daunting. Perhaps Alicia would help her. Even as she thought it she scolded herself. He was looking after her horse, not Alicia's.

"I appreciate it, ma'am." He started to leave, then turned back, fishing in a pocket. He brought out a button and held it out to her. She let him place it in the palm of her hand. He tipped his hat and marched away.

She found a place to stow the basket and went back to Alicia. "He's gone," she said. "Won't you come out now?"

Alicia shook her head. She sat on the edge of the bed, her hands folded primly on her lap.

"But it's hot in here."

Alicia shook her head again. "Someone will see me," she whispered.

"You can stay in the back of the tent, in the shadows. You need to get some air."

Alicia relented. She followed Rebecca into the main room but moved the chair to the back corner where she could easily slip into the bedroom.

"Now," Rebecca said, feeling as if she had solved one problem and was ready to tackle another, "tell me what you want me to bring from Father's tent."

Before Alicia could answer, her eyes grew big and she scurried behind the curtain.

Rebecca turned to find Paddy Malone with his hand raised ready to knock on the tent post. "I see ye have company, ma'am."

"It's only my cousin," Rebecca said. It was a good thing Aunt Belle hadn't stuck around a little longer, she thought. There had been a steady stream of men at her tent all morning, though all for innocent reasons.

"Ah. I've eggs for ye, ma'am." He fished two out of his pockets. "I'll be back another time."

"She'll be staying here until Clark's detachment returns," Rebecca added softly. "You can trust her to keep your secret."

He seemed to consider it a moment. "I'll be around on Sunday, then," he whispered. He touched his forehead and sauntered away.

Rebecca put the eggs on the straw in the crate of dishes and turned back to glare at the empty chair. Alicia was just shy about her current appearance. When the cuts healed a little, she would be her old self again. Or so she hoped.

Rebecca and Alicia settled into a comfortable routine. Mornings, Whiting came by and shared breakfast with Rebecca, bringing whatever news he had heard. Once he was gone, the women opened the front portion of their tent, to keep it from becoming stiflingly hot. Alicia stayed deep in the shadows but, Rebecca reasoned, she got some fresh air anyway.

Hank brought meat and danced. Rebecca tried to get Alicia to join them, thinking a dance with the boy would revive her spirits, but Alicia adamantly refused.

Independence Day brought a small celebration. With the fort under construction and the constant threat of Indian trouble, nothing elaborate had been planned. Rebecca and Alicia didn't attend what little activities took place. Without Clark, Rebecca saw no reason to celebrate.

Belle visited every day. She would begin by being sympathetic to poor Alicia and end by being angry. She couldn't understand why Alicia didn't simply pretend that nothing had happened and behave accordingly. "I daresay if nobody knows, it can hardly matter," she said once as she was leaving. "A prospective husband would have to be told, I suppose. But there's time enough to worry about that."

On Sunday morning, when Clark had been gone for nearly a week, Belle arrived dressed to attend the chaplain's services. Alicia refused to attend with her.

"But your cuts hardly show," Belle said. "We'll tell them you took a fall."

"I don't want to tell anybody anything," Alicia said, turning her sad eyes on Rebecca.

"You go ahead, Aunt Belle. You can tell them I have a stomach complaint."

"And have everyone in the fort coming by to ask after you?" Belle countered. "I dare say you'd be calling far more attention to yourself and therefore to Alicia if you *don't* come.''

In the end, Alicia gave in. A few minutes later, Rebecca, her hand firmly locked in Alicia's, strolled casually toward the open-air chapel. She realized that she had hardly left the tent in a week.

They arrived just as the chaplain was ready to begin and found seats in the back row. Alicia sat at rigid attention but relaxed as the service progressed. Rebecca decided that Belle had done the right thing by insisting that Alicia come.

The congregation had just begun the last hymn when a commotion caught Rebecca's attention. Troops were coming in. Clark! Without a thought to propriety, she left her place and ran to meet them.

Her father had left the service as well; she discovered him hurrying along beside her. They intercepted the troops near the corral. Two things registered on Rebecca's mind at the same time. None of the soldiers was Clark, and one saddle carried a covered body.

She hung back, fighting terror, as the second lieutenant approached the colonel.

''Lieutenant Forrester sent us back, sir,'' the soldier said.

Rebecca nearly wilted with relief. She took a deep breath hoping to get her heart back to its natural rhythm.

''We tried to take the deserter alive, sir, but he

made it impossible. Lieutenant Forrester said he needed to be returned to the fort, to Dr. Garman and wouldn't let us bury him.''

The lieutenant was clearly bewildered by the order but knew better than to ask for an explanation. Rumors of a plague might go flying, but Alicia's secret was safe.

"Where the hell's Forrester, then?" the colonel asked. Rebecca's question exactly, though she might have phrased it a little differently.

"We met up with Lieutenant Colonel Custer, sir. He was supposed to rendezvous with Lieutenant Kidder of the Second but Kidder never arrived. He's trying to pick up Kidder's trail, and Lieutenant Forrester and the rest of our detachment joined the search. Custer's had forty-three desertions, sir.''

Rebecca's father dismissed the officer. He turned to Rebecca and sighed. "Clark'll be all right.''

She nodded. She didn't like Clark riding under the command of someone who would inspire so many men to desert.

"Don't look so sad, girl. He caught the bastard and killed him, too. Alicia won't have to suffer through a trial. Let's go give her the good news.''

Better news came later that day when Dr. Garman paid them a visit. He checked Alicia's cuts and declared them healed.

"Now," he said, getting down to the real reason for his visit, "this young man they brought in this morning, Private Brooks, is he the one who attacked you?''

Alicia nodded. Rebecca moved closer to her, ready to offer support.

"I'm certain you needn't be concerned about disease. Should we still worry about a baby?''

Alicia shook her head.

Dr. Garman's old face broke into a smile. "Good then. All that's left to do is regain your strength and your spirit. For the first, I prescribe strolls around the fort. As for the second, the best thing to do is find someone who needs your help.''

In the days that followed, Alicia and Rebecca fell back into their old routine, except Rebecca insisted Alicia follow the doctor's advice and take a walk every day. They went early in the morning before the heat of the day, and while there were few people about. Alicia no longer hid whenever anyone arrived, though she was clearly nervous around men.

When Hank came, she joined in the singing and laughed at Rebecca's efforts to teach Hank more complicated and faster dances. She would offer advice, but refused to take a turn at the dancing.

Sergeant Whiting's arm healed, and he was put back on the active list. His leisurely breakfasts with Rebecca ended, but he managed to find a minute nearly every day to stop and ask after the women.

He always had a bit of gossip and occasionally real news.

In mid-July, Sergeant Whiting reported that cholera had broken out at Fort Harker. "The fort's been evacuated," he said.

Rebecca and Alicia were sitting in the shade in front of the tent. Whiting had refused the chair but squatted nearby to talk. Rebecca caught some note of hesitation in his voice and asked, "Evacuated...to here?"

"Yes, ma'am, that's what I heard."

Whiting couldn't stay and left them to mull over the news. Rebecca wondered how poor old Dr. Garman would handle the load. Of course, there could be another doctor on staff, she hadn't been near the hospital tents to find out, nor had she any reason to have asked.

Alicia's voice interrupted her thoughts. "Maybe that's who needs my help."

Rebecca turned toward her young cousin, not wanting to guess what she was thinking. "Who?"

"The sick soldiers when they get here."

"Alicia. Do you know what cholera is like? Nearly half the people who get it die."

Alicia shrugged. "Maybe they won't if there's enough help."

Rebecca left her chair and knelt beside Alicia. "They," she said, trying to keep her voice calm. "Alicia, I'm talking about you."

"Rebecca," she answered quietly, "I need to find some reason to live so I'll quit wanting to die."

"Don't even say things like that."

"It's true, Rebecca. All my dreams were ruined that night. I'll never have a husband, a family. I can't even stand to have a man talk to me."

"But that'll pass, Alicia. You've gotten much braver the last few days."

Alicia shook her head. "You don't know. I feel so sick inside. It's more than fear. Once, when you were gone, somebody, I don't know who, came looking for you. I thought he was— I mean, he even looked like—"

"Alicia." Rebecca tried to pull her cousin into her arms, but Alicia pushed her away.

"I have to finish. I hid, but this terrible panic came over me anyway. He went away, but I still wanted to run. It didn't completely pass until you came home."

"But how can you think of going off to work in the hospital?"

"Dr. Garman doesn't frighten me. And I don't think the sick soldiers will either. I know they can't hurt me."

Rebecca wanted to scream at her cousin's logic. "They *can* hurt you, Alicia. They can make *you* sick, too. They'll be quarantined. You probably won't be allowed to come back here until the epidemic's over."

"You don't need me here, Rebecca."

"What about your mother? Do you think she's going to allow this?"

"I won't ask her. I have to do this." She rose from her seat and Rebecca stood as well. "I'll go talk to Dr. Garman."

"I'll come with you."

"You won't talk me out of this," Alicia said as they started toward the hospital tent.

"Maybe I'll volunteer as well." Rebecca hoped Dr. Garman would help her talk Alicia out of the idea. The work would be discouraging and exhausting as well as dangerous. But if Alicia insisted, Rebecca would be there to watch over her.

Dr. Garman's reaction wasn't at all what Rebecca had hoped. "Why, Alicia, this could be just the thing for both of us," he said. "You may find your life's work."

"Or your life's end," Rebecca said, growing desperate for an argument that worked.

"Ah, but we're not so ignorant of cholera as we were twenty years ago. It's caused by a contaminated water supply. The only case we've had here so far is a soldier just in from the field."

A case here already. Whiting hadn't mentioned that. "If it's so safe," Rebecca said, "I'll help as well."

Dr. Garman shook his head. "You have a young husband who'll be coming home soon. You'll want to leave the quarantine tent and could well pass the disease on to him, tired and weak as he's likely to be."

She couldn't quite imagine her husband weak, but it was simply a fleeting thought, and her brain returned to the matter at hand. "Then how can you promise Alicia will be perfectly safe?"

The doctor was unperturbed by the outburst. "I can't promise. But she hasn't ever been perfectly safe, has she?"

Rebecca gave up on the doctor and turned back to Alicia. Though she had been quiet during the exchange, her chin jutted out at a determined angle. Without another word, Rebecca admitted defeat.

"When should I start?" Alicia asked.

"There's much to do before the soldiers get here sometime tomorrow. They'll all be separated from the other troops for a few days. But there are bound to be some afflicted with the disease when they arrive. I'd appreciate your help as soon as you're willing to give it."

"I'll go pack a few things," Alicia said.

The doctor nodded. "We'll have a place ready for you."

Rebecca watched Alicia as she packed. "What am I going to tell your mother?" she asked.

"You probably better tell her the truth," Alicia said. "She's likely to catch you in a lie."

Rebecca scowled. "I mean, how am I going to explain this to her? She's going to be upset."

"She's always upset, Rebecca. You should be used to it by now. Will you walk with me to the hospital?"

"No." Maybe the thought of walking across the camp on her own would make her realize how foolish she was being. She certainly wouldn't have thought of doing it the day before.

"Then this is goodbye," Alicia said.

Rebecca let her hug her. She let her leave the tent. She even gave her a full two minutes before she ran to catch up. "I'll walk with you," she said.

"Don't keep trying to change my mind."

Rebecca shook her head. "No, I know stubborn when I crash into it."

"Good," Alicia said, smiling up at her, "because I feel better than I have in weeks."

She did look more like her old self, Rebecca conceded.

They said their goodbyes again at the hospital. Dr. Garman assured Rebecca that she could visit Alicia outside the tent. "There's very little chance of spreading the disease without direct contact," he said.

Rebecca stopped at her father's tent to give the news to Belle. After moaning, yelling and crying, she finally accepted her daughter's decision. She said, however, that she would never forgive Rebecca if Alicia died.

Rebecca went home drained by the confrontation. She sank into one of the chairs in front of her tent, feeling lonely. How long before Clark got home? It had been more than a week since there had been any word.

She did her best to shake off the worry. She had enough concern with Alicia. She would have to trust Clark to look after himself.

The next day, Sergeant Whiting stopped by at noon. Rebecca was roasting a chunk of venison. Hank had brought down a deer and practically made himself rich by selling what his mother didn't want to dry.

"Where's your little cousin?" Whiting asked.

Rebecca frowned. "She's decided to become a nurse."

"A nurse? I see." He squatted across the fire from her. "She's volunteered to help with the epidemic. They came in this morning, you know."

Rebecca nodded. "Don't tell me you think it's a good idea."

"She's kindhearted. Maybe she felt she had to help."

Rebecca glared at him. "To make matters worse, I tried to volunteer too so I could watch over her, and the doctor refused my help. Maybe the doctor knows I'm not kindhearted."

Whiting laughed. "I think you're kindhearted. You looked after your cousin when she was hurt."

Rebecca's head came up. "Who told you she was hurt?"

Whiting raised a hand as if to ward off the question. "I just put things together. Her behavior, the deserter, Clark's request to check in on the two of you.

"Besides, I wasn't talking about Alicia, I was talking about you. You like to tease and joke and laugh, and none of those poor sick boys would get any rest. You're nothing like Annie, that's for sure."

The smile would have died on Rebecca's lips if she hadn't forced it to stay in place. She turned the spit that held the meat and hoped her question sounded only mildly curious. "Who's Annie?"

"Annie," Whiting said with a laugh, "was your lieutenant's girlfriend. She's nice enough, I guess, but she isn't full of life the way you are. I gotta go. Take care of yourself."

Rebecca forced herself to smile up at him as he rose and left. She watched her lunch cook, then char and finally burst into flames while a thousand questions raced across her brain. And the decision she had to make became clearer.

Chapter Fourteen

The tent city ahead appeared to reflect the last colors of the sunrise, and Clark thought for a moment he was hallucinating. It seemed incredible that they had left Fort Wallace little more than two days before. Custer had set a grueling pace and planned to move on today with fresh horses for his seventy-five hand-picked men. Clark counted himself lucky not to be one of them.

Custer ordered his bugler to play "When Johnny Comes Marching Home." It brought every unoccupied resident of the fort out to see them ride in.

Clark found Rebecca, her skirt clutched in one hand as she hurried toward the command tent. She slowed occasionally to scan the troops. When she found him she smiled and waved. He returned the greeting. For a moment he could pretend that everything was right between them.

At the corral, the troops dismounted, and Clark

turned his mount over to his sergeant. He followed Custer and his junior officers to Huntington's tent. He passed so close to Rebecca he couldn't resist reaching out to touch her. There wasn't time to pull her into his arms, and he contented himself with the brush of his fingers against hers.

Custer's audience with Huntington was brief, the former being eager to be on his way. But Huntington asked Clark to remain and give his own report of the nearly three weeks since he had left the fort. In return, Huntington told Clark about the troops from Fort Harker that had arrived the day before.

"We heard of the epidemic, sir," Clark said. "I suspect Lieutenant Colonel Custer is worried about his wife back at Fort Riley. This trip to Fort Harker for supplies for Fort Wallace is Custer's own idea."

Huntington grinned. "You think he'll head on to Fort Riley?"

"I wouldn't be completely surprised, sir."

Huntington waved the subject away. "It's good you're home, Clark. Belle says she's caught your wife entertaining gentlemen callers twice, now."

This shouldn't have been a complete surprise either, but Clark felt as if he had been kicked in the gut. All the air had rushed from his lungs, and he didn't trust his voice.

"One was Sergeant Whiting and the other was our striker, Paddy Malone."

Clark took a deep breath, easing some of the pain.

"I asked Sergeant Whiting to check on her and your niece while I was away." He wished he had an easy explanation for Malone.

"Well, you know Belle. It could all be innocent enough. I wouldn't recommend you confront Rebecca with it. That girl can turn things around until you feel guilty for asking."

Colonel Huntington's assessment of Rebecca never quite fit with his own, but arguing with his commanding officer didn't come naturally. Besides, he had a feeling he wouldn't get anywhere if he did. His response was the one that came most easily to his tongue. "Yes, sir."

Huntington nodded. "You're dismissed."

Clark left the tent. He wasn't sure which was more upsetting, the news of the male callers or the way the colonel talked about his daughter. He had half hoped she would still be waiting outside but the area was deserted.

He headed for his tent, trying to decide what, if anything, he should do about Belle's rumors. Regardless, things couldn't continue as they were. He and Rebecca needed to talk. But what could he say? He was so tired after Custer's forced march he would probably end up begging her to love him.

Tomorrow, he decided, after a good night's sleep. If that was possible next to Rebecca.

As he neared his tent he heard Rebecca humming a slow soft melody. The front of the tent was open, and he saw them as he stopped. Rebecca and Hank Raymond, locked in an embrace. His gut took another blow.

When the buzzing in his ears subsided and the haze left his vision, he realized they weren't kissing. They were dancing.

"I like the fast ones better, Mrs. Forrester. I don't feel like your little feet are in quite as much danger."

"But when you're dancing fast and *do* step on my toes, you step down harder."

"Really?"

"Trust me."

Clark leaned against the tent post to watch them. Rebecca's humming was slightly breathless. The glimpses he got of her face revealed cheeks pink from the heat. He could see she was smiling and discovered he was as well. The Raymond boy's back was to him, and Clark could only guess he was enthralled.

"You're awfully nice to teach me to dance, Mrs. Forrester," Hank said. "I promise I'll use everything you've taught me."

"I need the exercise. All the meat you bring would make me fat without the lessons." She stepped away, ending the dance.

Clark clapped briefly, bringing both dancers around to face him.

"Clark!"

"Lieutenant Forrester!"

Clark smiled. "I didn't mean to startle you."

"We were...I was...ah...leaving." The boy slipped past and headed for home.

Rebecca hadn't moved. She watched him closely, and he wondered what she expected to see. "Dancing lessons?" She nodded. "Did you think I'd be upset?"

She shrugged and looked away. He had the feeling she was disappointed. Because he had brought the dancing to an end? He tried to dismiss the thought; Hank was just a boy. But Rebecca was young, too.

"I'm going to the creek for a swim," he said. It was on the tip of his tongue to invite her along, but he wasn't so exhausted that he wouldn't respond to her, and he didn't trust his control right now.

"I'll fix some lunch while you're gone," she said, already making herself busy.

Clark went to his trunk for soap and clean clothes. He hesitated a moment before leaving. There should be something he could say, something that would express part of what he was feeling without leaving his heart open to too much pain.

I missed you. But he didn't say it aloud. He was almost out the tent when she stopped him.

"Clark, I'm glad you're home."

He nodded and left, unable to say what he wanted to. He had never known he was a coward before, but there was no other explanation. In the morning, he told himself. He wanted to wait until his head was clearer. But he knew that was only half the truth.

Clark felt a little better when he returned from the creek. While he was hot again almost instantly, the layer of grime was gone. But the cold water didn't seem to sharpen his wits. He was still feeling cowardly and confused when he approached his tent.

And watched a man step out of it. "Private Powers?"

"Sir." The man tucked a bundle under his arm and saluted. "I heard you were back."

"Were you looking for me?"

"No, I was—" He had raised a hand toward the tent and seemed to realize suddenly how his presence could be construed. "I've been looking after your wife's horse in exchange for my mending."

Clark nodded, though he wasn't sure he understood. He watched Powers walk away then turned into the tent. Rebecca was setting the table and seemed oblivious to the exchange.

"Why is Mr. Powers looking after your horse?"

"It seemed the best way to insure that he was cared for."

Clark walked toward her. She hadn't yet looked at him. "I thought you would want to do that yourself. I don't object. I'm just surprised," he added quickly.

"I could, of course." She hesitated. "The truth is I got spoiled by the pants."

"Then wear the pants."

She shook her head. "People wouldn't understand. I've got some lunch ready."

She brushed past him and bent to lift a pan from the fire. He remembered her little backside clad in the wool uniform. He was smiling when she turned to face him. She seemed surprised and a little flustered.

"When did you start caring what other people thought?" He followed her to the table less from hunger than from a desire to be a little closer to her. Her dark curls had grown out since he had cut them, and he wondered what they felt like.

She slid into one of the chairs, slipping out of his reach. "When it became more than my own reputation at stake."

It sounded rehearsed. Or as if she were trying to convince herself. "You're not concerned what visits from Mr. Powers or young Raymond will do to your reputation. Or mine."

She looked up at him, her eyes wide.

"Don't look so horrified," he said quickly. "I know why they were here. And I'm sure you have an explanation for Mr. Malone's visits, as well."

He hadn't meant to mention Malone but, God forgive him, he was jealous. Though he tried not to let it show.

"He gives me eggs in exchange for..."

He raised an eyebrow as he waited.

"It's a secret," she said.

He shook his head. "Not from me."

He thought he saw a hint of a smile in her eyes. She leaned forward and said just above a whisper, "He can't read. I've been writing letters for him."

Her father had been right. He felt guilty for asking. He dipped up some of the fried potatoes and put them on his plate. He wanted to ask if that covered all her male callers, but maybe he was happier not knowing. Rebecca changed the subject, and he hoped that didn't mean she had something to hide.

"Tell me the news," she said. "Did you find Kidder's men?"

"We found their bodies." The picture came to Clark's mind and he tried to brush it away. They had picked up the trail, then found a dead horse and finally the mutilated bodies.

"I'm sorry," Rebecca said.

"It was too small a group to send out. They made an easy target. Ten troopers, one Sioux scout, and Kidder, with a wagon-load of supplies." He couldn't help but think of their own expedition with several wagons and an escort of forty untried men. They had been lucky.

"Any other news?" she asked.

"Your father says there's talk of a peace commission being sent out from Washington."

"More treaties to break?"

As Clark's hunger was satisfied, he felt weariness

overtaking him. He could hear it in his voice when he answered, "It's got to be better than this."

"You need to sleep," she said gently, reaching across the table to rest her hand on his.

He wanted to lift her fingers to his mouth, wanted to pull her into his arms. Wanted, he realized, more than he was capable of at that moment. "Why don't you go for a ride while I catch up on lost sleep?"

She hesitated and he added, "Wear the pants if you want."

Her smile was shy but he pretended it was teasing and flirtatious, and he let it fuel his imagination as he stumbled off to bed. He was asleep almost instantly.

When Clark awoke it was dark. He didn't need a light to know Rebecca slept beside him. Right beside him. He supposed she had gotten used to sleeping in the middle of the bed while he was gone, then remembered Alicia had been here when he left. Perhaps she had only stayed a day or so. The colonel had told him that Alicia was working at the hospital so he had assumed she was fine and hadn't asked Rebecca about her.

It was just as well. If he didn't *know* how long she had stayed, he could imagine she had been here until recently. Then he could pretend Rebecca was cuddled against him because she wanted to be near him. She had thrown one leg over his because she had missed him and wanted to remind herself that he was home. He didn't want to know better.

He had gone to bed fully clothed but even through the fabric of his pants, he could tell she hadn't. He couldn't help letting his hand inch toward the delicious weight on his thigh. His fingers contacted warm bare skin. He assumed there was a gown bunched somewhere above this expanse of leg. But he pretended there wasn't.

He wanted to run his hand along her leg, up and over her hip, but he didn't dare. It would wake her. Would she jump away, shocked? Or roll away, bored? Either way, it would ruin the fantasy. As long as she slept undisturbed, he could pretend she would cuddle closer, return the caress, open her lips to his kiss.

From there his mind imagined all sorts of possibilities. His body willingly responded. When the ache reached a point where he was afraid he would give in to temptation, he carefully extricated himself from his wife and slipped into the other room.

He took a match from his pocket and struck it, finding a lamp to light. He kept the wick low, not wanting the light to bother Rebecca. A quick check of his pocket watch told him he had slept nearly fifteen hours. It was early, but he couldn't return to the bed.

Unless there was an emergency, he was off duty today. He wasn't sure what he would do to fill the hours, but it seemed he was getting an early start. Outside, he rekindled the fire, started coffee and put water on to heat so he could shave. He was inside, mixing the slivers of soap in the warm water when he felt Rebecca slip past the curtain.

"You're up early," she said.

"So are you, now. Did the light bother you?"

She shrugged. "It doesn't matter. I want to talk to you."

"All right." He left the brush in the cup and turned, giving her his attention.

She smiled. "It can wait until you're through shaving."

He studied her for a moment before he turned to the mirror he had hung on the tent post and began lathering his face. He needed to talk to her, too, only he wasn't sure what to say. He was happy to put it off, even for a few minutes. Maybe the right words would come to him.

"Do you mind if I watch?" she asked.

She had moved closer until he could see her in the corner of his vision. "I don't mind."

"I like watching you shave."

"I know." He set the cup aside and lifted the razor. He turned to her as he spoke. "You watched me nearly every morning when we were on the trail."

Her cheeks turned rosy under his gaze. He pulled his eyes back to the mirror. She hadn't realized he knew about her morning visits to his camp. He probably shouldn't have told her. But this morning was the time for honesty.

She was quiet until he dropped the razor in the pan of water, splashed a little on his face and reached for the towel. She took the towel when he was finished and wiped away a bit of soap from his ear he would have sworn wasn't there when he looked in the mirror.

"What did you want to talk about?" he asked.

"I've been thinking," she began, turning to move a few steps away. Abruptly she faced him. "I want to go back to Chicago."

"Chicago?" He was nearly holding his breath. "Do you have friends there you want to visit?"

She shook her head. "I'll go to stay."

Bewildered, he tried again. "I know life is hard here, but the tent's only temporary. Things will get—"

She cut him off. "That's not it."

Whatever was bothering her she seemed reluctant to tell him. He didn't even want to guess. The dark corners of the tent made him think of how dark and barren his life would be without her. With a sense of desperation he said, "I thought you liked the prairie."

"I do, Clark." She took a deep breath and he held his. "I know about Annie."

He heard the nearly forgotten name with a shock.

"Annie? Rebecca, I swear I haven't seen Annie since before I met you."

"I know. I know," she said quickly. She seemed on the verge of tears. "That's why I'm going to leave."

She hung her head, and Clark moved to take her in his arms. "I'm lost, Rebecca."

She slipped out of reach and paced across the tent. "My aunt told me about...a man's...well, his needs. And if I'm gone you can go back to Annie."

Clark blinked at the narrow back, certain he didn't understand. "You're leaving me, so I can take a mistress?"

The curls bobbed as she nodded.

It was too ridiculous to believe. There were many arguments against it, not the least of which was his own desire to be with Rebecca, not Annie. He asked the only thing he could think of that wouldn't leave his heart bare before her. "What is your father going to think about this?"

She spun around. "Father! I'd forgotten about him."

The situation might be comical if his life wasn't at stake. "I find him hard to forget."

She took another deep breath and let it out slowly. He tried not to be distracted by the way the nightgown tightened across the soft swell of her breasts.

"All right," she said, as if giving in to something. "I'll stay. But please be discreet."

Clark was ready to put an end to this foolishness, but he still didn't know what had led up to it, what she really wanted. "Rebecca," he began, moving toward her. "With Annie, I thought I was discreet, but you found out about her, anyway."

She sighed, looking completely discouraged. He put his hands on her shoulders, grateful that she didn't move away. "What Annie and I had was over before I went east. She married someone else, and I'm happy for her. Now, please tell me what this is about."

She looked up at him, her eyes bright with tears. "You've been around me enough to know how selfish I am. I wanted you and it never occurred to me that you might not want me, too. All I knew was that I loved you, then I ruined your life."

She choked on the last word, and one tear escaped to run down her cheek. Still she fought to keep from crying.

She had said she loved him. He wanted to kiss her soundly and put off the rest of the conversation until later, but he knew she needed to understand. And he couldn't let her continue to believe he thought she was selfish.

"Rebecca," he whispered, "you married me to save my career. I shouldn't have let you." Her lips trembled, and she nodded. "That's not what I meant. I let you because I was too in love with you to resist."

She blinked, her tears drying. "You love me?" Her cheeks turned rosy as she asked, "Then why didn't you *do* something?" One little fist struck him in the ribs.

He tried to keep from grinning. "You quit teasing me. You never flirted. I thought you had grown tired of me."

"I was trying to be a perfect wife."

He couldn't hold back the laugh. She looked a little offended. "I'm afraid my idea of a perfect wife isn't quite the same as yours."

"So, describe the perfect wife, and it better not be Annie."

"No," he said, laughing. "I got a glimpse of the perfect wife when we were playing chess."

"When I beat you?" she asked, grinning finally.

"When your eyes sparkled just like they're doing now. When you teased and tempted me." He drew her closer. "When you kissed me."

He bent and took her lips. She responded immediately, wrapping her arms around him, pressing herself against him. He drew out the kiss until he felt her tremble. He raised his head and whispered, "Do you want me?"

"Yes," she breathed.

He bent and scooped her into his arms. "You wouldn't be teasing me, would you?"

She giggled, clinging to his neck. "Maybe you better find out."

"I intend to." He carried her across the tent. She swept the curtain out of the way, and he laid her on the bed. "Did you know you curled up beside me while you slept?" he asked, crawling in beside her.

"I dreamed you pulled me into your arms while I slept."

"Did I?" he asked, pulling her into his arms.

"And then you ran your hands up my legs," she whispered.

"Like this?" He slipped his hand under her gown and slid it up to her hip. "Then what?"

"Then I woke up." Her voice was breathless.

He sighed. "Too bad. I was hoping to be your dream come true."

"You are." She brought her hands up between them and unbuttoned his shirt. "You really love me?"

"Don't ever doubt it." It was dark and he wanted to see her, but he contented himself with letting his hands explore her body. He had seen her once before and remembered every detail. In a moment she was pushing his shirt off his shoulders, and he was tugging at her gown. They traded chores and tossed all their clothes aside.

She seemed as curious as he and let her fingers trail over his back, his ribs and lower. She found his swollen member, her touch easing his longing and tightening the tension at the same time.

"Do you like me to touch you?" she asked.

"Yes," he managed. He fondled a soft breast, feeling the nipple harden, trying to control the desire that was increasing rapidly with her touch.

She groaned and he echoed the sentiment. He wanted to plunge deep inside her. But he needed to be sure she was ready. He gently pulled her hand away. "We need to slow down a little," he said.

"Was I doing it wrong?"

The worry in her tone made him chuckle. "You were doing it too well. I want you to catch up."

He lowered his head and brought the peaked nipple into his mouth. She threw her arms back against the mattress and moaned. He lavished equal attention on the other breast while she arched against him.

When he was sure she was ready, he trailed his fingers down her belly. He stroked her curls for a moment before he sought entrance. He found her hot and wet.

She gasped at the intimate intrusion, and he took her lips in a hungry kiss. He urged her legs apart and settled over her. "Trust me?" he whispered in her ear.

She didn't answer but her arms wrapped around his neck and she clung to him. He eased into her, struck the barrier, and fought for control.

"Clark?" she whispered.

She was frightened, he thought. He had moved too quickly. He started to withdraw but she wrapped her legs around him. It was all the encouragement he needed. He thrust into her, heard her gasp, felt her nails press into his back.

"Did I hurt you?" he whispered.

"Hmm?" Her mouth was close to his ear. "I don't think so. The pain's gone now."

She squirmed under him and he moved, slowly at first, mindful of her needs. When he felt her plunge over the edge the last thread of control snapped. She muffled her cries in his neck, and he did his best to swallow his own.

After taking a moment to catch his breath he rolled off of her, pulling her into the crook of his arm.

"What will the neighbors think?" she whispered.

"They'll think it's about time."

"Oh, you," She gave him a mock punch in the ribs. "They haven't been listening for this. Have they?"

He laughed. "Maybe they're thinking they should have let their wives come this summer instead of waiting for their quarters to be built."

She sighed and snuggled closer. "Would we have done this sooner if I had flirted with you?"

"If you had so much as winked."

"I'll remember that in the future." She yawned.

"Go back to sleep," he urged softly.

"You won't leave?"

"I'll stay right here."

He let her sleep until there was light enough in the room for him to admire the curve of her cheek, the swell of her breasts, the shade of her lips and her nipples. Then he woke her. She didn't seem to mind.

They managed to spend the entire day close to the tent, a large portion of it in the bed. Rebecca sent Hank away, telling him Clark was exhausted from the recent campaign. Clark had chuckled over that, telling her campaigning wasn't what was keeping him in bed.

The following day, the lovers decided to venture out. Rebecca wanted to see that Alicia was all right, and Clark was worried that there would be rumors that he was ill. The last thing he wanted, he told her, was to be hauled off to the quarantine tent.

The orderly that met them at the hospital asked them to wait outside while he went to find Alicia. Rebecca found herself growing nervous as she waited. A few minutes later, when Alicia stepped outside, Rebecca wanted to run to her. Clark's arm, wrapped possessively around her waist, was all that stopped her.

"Are you all right, Alicia?" she asked.

Alicia nodded. "It's hard work but I've found people who need my help. So in a way it's wonderful."

"Do you need anything?"

Alicia shook her head. "Your father came to see me yesterday and asked the same thing."

Rebecca felt a pang of guilt. Yesterday, she hadn't

even thought of Alicia. "Should I come see you every day, in case you think of something?"

"Whenever you can. The days go fast here."

Rebecca wanted to cry for the Alicia that seemed to be lost forever. But this new mature Alicia would find her own way.

"I need to get back to work," Alicia said. "Thank you for coming." She turned and disappeared inside the tent.

Rebecca looked up to find Clark watching her. She gave him a brave smile.

"She'll be all right," he said.

"If she doesn't get sick."

"You can't protect her all her life."

Rebecca nodded and they turned to find her father headed their way. They waited for him to join them.

"Forrester," the colonel said, "it's good to see you up and about again."

"Thank you, sir." Rebecca thought he did a wonderful job keeping a straight face. She didn't even try.

"You looked pleased with yourself," he said, turning to Rebecca.

"Thank you, sir," she answered, mimicking her husband's accent.

The nod he gave her was surprisingly approving.

"Telegram just arrived," the colonel went on, turning back to Clark. "Congress approved the peace commission. We're to call all the troops in from the field.''

"So the war's over?" Rebecca asked.

Her father nodded and, with a squeeze to Rebecca's shoulder, moved on toward the hospital tent. Rebecca and Clark turned toward home. They could hear the colonel ordering the soldier to find his niece and send her out.

"Do you think it's safe to call back all the troops?" Rebecca asked as they walked.

"The Tenth is stationed all along the Smoky Hill and Santa Fe trails. They're in defensive positions, and surely they'll remain in place until the treaty is signed. Campaigns like Custer's have been fairly fruitless anyway."

"So, it means you're going to be home," Rebecca said, letting her voice turn seductive.

"I may get sent out in charge of a wood-cutting expedition."

"You better not be gone three weeks."

He turned her into his arms. "Sometime, I'll have to leave you again."

She looked up at him, and he buried his hands in her hair, framing her face with his palms. "You can take my heart with you," she said.

He smiled at her and kissed her lips quickly. "All the time I was gone, do you know what I carried next to my heart?"

She shook her head.

"Your hair."

She blinked up at him.

"After you talked me into cutting it, I wrapped it in a handkerchief and put it in the inside pocket of my uniform blouse. I was already in love with you, I think. You can check when you get home if you don't believe me."

She couldn't stop grinning at him. "If it's so precious, why aren't you carrying it now?"

"Because right now," he said, drawing her closer, "I have you."

Any other teasing comment slipped Rebecca's mind as his lips descended to claim hers.

* * * * *

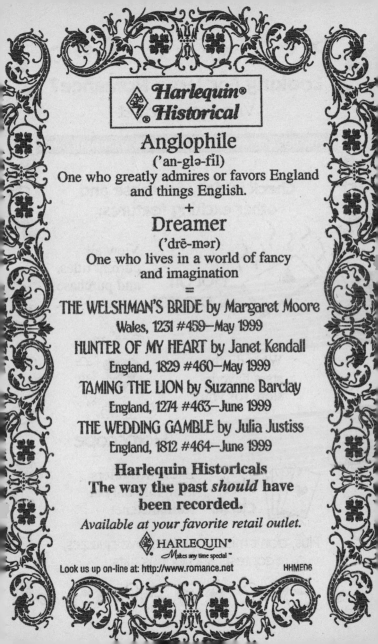

Harlequin® Historical

Anglophile

('an-glə-fīl)
One who greatly admires or favors England
and things English.

+

Dreamer

('drē-mər)
One who lives in a world of fancy
and imagination

=

THE WELSHMAN'S BRIDE by Margaret Moore
Wales, 1231 #459—May 1999

HUNTER OF MY HEART by Janet Kendall
England, 1829 #460—May 1999

TAMING THE LION by Suzanne Barclay
England, 1274 #463—June 1999

THE WEDDING GAMBLE by Julia Justiss
England, 1812 #464—June 1999

Harlequin Historicals
The way the past *should* have
been recorded.

Available at your favorite retail outlet.

HARLEQUIN®
Makes any time special™

COMING NEXT MONTH FROM

HARLEQUIN HISTORICALS